Amit Chaudhuri is the author of six highly acclaimed novels, including *The Immortals*, *A Strange and Sublime Address*, *Afternoon Raag* and *Freedom Song* which – between them – have won the Commonwealth Writers' Prize, the Betty Trask Prize, the Encore Award, the *Los Angeles Times* Book Prize for Fiction and the Sahitya Akademi Award. His most recent novel is *Odysseus Abroad*. He is also a poet, an acclaimed musician, a highly regarded critic, a Fellow of the Royal Society of Literature and Professor of Contemporary Literature at the University of East Anglia. In 2012 he was awarded the Infosys Prize for outstanding contribution to the humanities in literary studies. He lives in Calcutta and Norwich.

PRAISE FOR *A NEW WORLD*

'Chaudhuri holds our attention with unobtrusive evocation of place, texture and humanity. [He] is capable of producing that quicksilver compound of recognition and surprise, which is, of course, what so often distinguishes art from stage directions.'
Economist

'A gentle book of tremendous patience and sensitivity … Chaudhuri's beautiful fourth novel offers delicate tableaux vivants. It whispers its visions to us with an eerie intimacy and power … But what distinguishes *A New World* is not its narrative contours, but its repose.'
Times Literary Supplement

'A very clever, very successful piece of work. It is beautifully, quietly written. You read it thinking Amit Chaudhuri has hit the target … Here is a wonderful book in plain English, which deserves to be enthusiastically accepted.'
Spectator

'Beautifully balanced, affecting, truthful … Among the literary voices from India to have made themselves heard in this country over the past ten years, Amit Chaudhuri is one of the quietest but most impressive.'
Anne Chisholm, *Sunday Telegraph*

'As in all Chaudhuri's novels, a compulsive narrative is somehow generated from near-total eventlessness.'
Guardian

'Chaudhuri employs both art and risk ... the writing is lovely.'
New York Times Book Review

'Fiercely witty.'
Financial Times

'Brilliantly conveys the richness of Calcutta's teeming neighbourhoods. These beautifully drawn images alone make the book worth reading.'
Seattle Times

'Brings to life the countless domestic dramas that make up life in urban India. Chaudhuri's writing is spare, precise, detailed, and unsentimental.'
Boston Globe

'The brilliance of his words lies in their sheer simplicity. A skilful writer, he effortlessly blurs the boundary of time and space ... Chaudhuri's controlled writing, which is also very lyrical, firmly places him among the front-runners of contemporary Indo-Anglian writers.'
Asian Age

'This kind of writing gives even the most mundane details a force and meaning that resonate beyond the book and into the lives of its readers.'
Rocky Mountain News

Amit Chaudhuri

A New World

ONEWORLD

A Oneworld Book

First published in the United Kingdom by Picador in 2000

This paperback edition first published in Great Britain and Australia by
Oneworld Publications, 2015

ISBN 978-1-78074-623-4
ISBN 978-1-78074-624-1 (eBook)

Typeset by Eleven Arts, Delhi
Printed and bound in Great Britain by Clays Ltd.

Oneworld Publications
10 Bloomsbury Street
London WC1B 3SR
England

To Rinka;
and our daughter,
Radha

He had come back in April, the aftermath of the lawsuit and court proceedings in two countries still fresh, the voices echoing behind him. But he felt robust.

'Here,' he said to the taxi driver that day in April—it was a Tuesday—when he arrived. His son was staring out of the window, as if a taxi were the most natural place to be in, apparently unaffected by its rusting window-edges and its noise. It was eleven o'clock in the morning; it should be ten o'clock now the previous night in America.

'Stop here,' said Jayojit to the taxi driver. 'Kitna hua?' he asked.

Vikram—that was his son's name, his maternal grandfather's choice—said, 'Are we here, baba?'

Though they spoke to each other in English, both Jayojit and his wife (ex-wife now? but she had still not married the man she was living with) had decided to retain, as far as their son was concerned, the Bengali appellations for mother and father: 'ma' and 'baba'. Ironical, thought Jayojit—he thought about these questions more and more these days; indeed, he could often *hear* himself thinking—that we did not think to teach him, at least

1

in practice, the other things that surround those words in our culture. He himself had learnt those meanings from the lives of his parents. It was curious how often he returned to his childhood and growing up these days, involuntarily, to their apparently random and natural sequence.

'Seventy-five rupees,' said the driver, turning his head and smiling; the man hadn't shaved for a few days. It was as if the taxi were his home and he had long not stepped out of it.

'Seventy-five rupees,' repeated Jayojit with a chuckle, while the driver smiled with a strange but recognizable demureness; the coyness of a struggler taking something extra from a person he considers well-to-do. Jayojit knew, from glancing at the numbers that had appeared on the meter, that he was paying more than he was supposed to, but he silently rummaged the new rupee notes in his wallet; he had changed fifty dollars at the airport.

'Yes, Bonny, we're here,' he proclaimed cheerfully to his son; Bonny was his pet name, given him by Jayojit's mother, a strange Western affectation from the old days, to call children names like these—though his mother was not westernized. The boy, his pale face red with the heat, with one or two darker streaks—evidence of the journey, of plane seats, uncomfortable positions, attempts to sleep—on his cheeks, was looking quietly at the gates. A sound, oddly lazy but determined, of a plank of wood being hit again and again, could be heard. The watchman at the gates of the multi-storeyed building and the indolent, shabby chauffeurs of the private cars, lounging in the shade, their backs leaning against their cars' bonnets, seemed to be intent on watching the occupants of the taxi and listening to that sound.

'E lo,' said Jayojit, handing the driver the money, who took it and began to count the notes. Experimentally pulling the lever that opened the door, he said to his son, 'Bonny, that's the way to do it.'

They had come with one heavy suitcase and a large shoulder bag slung around Jayojit's neck; in one hand he was carrying an Apple laptop and a one-litre bottle of Chivas Regal in a duty-free bag. The boy was wearing a bright-blue t-shirt and shorts, and on his back there was a kind of rucksack; he walked with the mournful loping air of a miniature expeditioner. The two or three part-time maidservants who always sat by the entrance steps looked at the two arrivers casually; it was as if they were used to the sight of huge itineraries, arrivals, and departures, and it no longer disturbed the monotony and fixedness of their lives. A faint smell of stale clothes and hair-oil came from them. Jayojit was a big man, five feet eleven, and fair-complexioned and still handsome in a bullish way; he was wearing a red t-shirt and off-white trousers on which the creases showed, and two Bangladesh Biman boarding cards stuck out from his shirt pocket.

The flat was on the fourth floor, number 14; a long corridor led to it, and then became a kind of verandah before it and its neighbouring flat. The nameplate on the door said 'Ananda Chatterjee'. He pressed the doorbell, which was really a buzzer with a prolonged droning sound which he associated with an immemorial middle-class constrictedness; and his son stood

3

facing the door, staring at the one-inch ledge at the bottom. It was Jayojit's mother who opened the door; immediately, upon opening it, her face, a rainbow of late morning light and shadows, of tiredness and alacrity, lit up with a smile, and she said: 'You've come, Joy!'

'Yes, ma,' he said jovially, and bent his big body to touch, in one of the awkward but anachronistic gestures that defined this family, her feet.

'You've put on weight, have you,' she said. 'There, let it be.' Then looking at Vikram she smiled, widening her mouth, so that her teeth showed, and said: 'Esho shona,' and then, remembering he might want her to speak in English, 'Come to thamma.' For the first time Vikram smiled.

Admiral Chatterjee was sitting inside on the sofa—a heart condition and diabetes had made him slow; but he was a big man too. He looked like a sailor, his longish grey hair and beard suggesting voyages, deck-parties, and a sea breeze; a painting by a minor artist, bought many years ago for five hundred rupees, hung behind him.

'How was the trip, Joy?' he boomed as he got to his feet. 'All right?'

They—Jayojit and his father—communicated, except for a few words and sentences, in English, establishing a rapport, a bluff friendship, which excluded the tenderness of the mother-son relationship—the latter finding expression in the mother's homely, slightly irritating Bengali, and talk centred round questions such as whether her son was hungry, or whether he had had a bath.

'Bloody taxi driver took extra money from me,' said Jayojit with a large smile, and then bent to touch his father's feet. 'Pranam karo, Bonny,' he said. The boy, who had been slipping off his rucksack so he might put it on a chair, interrupted himself, turned to walk gravely but obediently, with a light-footed sneaker-tread, towards his grandfather, to touch his feet.

'Let it be, let it be, dadu,' said the grandfather, who always seemed a little uncomfortable with others, whatever the situation. To his wife he said, 'Ruby, give the child something to eat!'

It was not easy to be intimate or relaxed with the Admiral. He was one of those men who, after Independence, had inherited the colonial's authority and position, his club cuisine and table manners, his board meetings and discipline; all along he had bullied his wife for not being as much a memsahib as he was a sahib. She had adored and feared him, of course, and paled beside him. Only before two things had he become strangely Bengali and native. The first was his in-laws; in those days when his wife and he still quarrelled and his in-laws were alive, his wife, crying softly, would pack her things and go away for a week to her parents' house; and he would be left dumbstruck, unable to say anything. The second was his grandson—Vikram; Bonny. He could not reconcile himself to the fact that the boy had to tag along part of the year with Jayojit, and then go back to his mother, who was living elsewhere on the vast American map, with someone else. He could not comprehend the loneliness of the child, or why the loneliness needed to exist. Yet, in spite of this, and in spite of the fact that the old India had changed, and he himself had grown somewhat decrepit, the official air still hung around him, like a presentiment.

Jayojit's mother disappeared into the kitchen, while Vikram said pleadingly to his father, not very loud:

'Baba, I'm not hungry!' There was a faint American broadening in the child's vowels.

'Baba, he's right—we've been eating *con*stantly on the plane— eating and sitting. Our body-clock's gone *com*pletely awry!'

'Have a bath, then, you two,' said Jayojit's father.

The heat had just begun to become intolerable—it was the middle of April. Outside, birds cried continuously, sharp, clear, obstinate cries. Shadows of windows and façades had settled everywhere upon parapets and bannisters.

'What we need,' said Jayojit, 'is a glass of water. Of course,' a look of exaggerated caution appeared on his face, 'as long as the water is boiled.'

'You've never drunk anything but boiled water since you were a child,' remonstrated his mother gently, returning with two glasses whose sides had already misted over. 'And you know your father always drinks boiled water.'

'Still, it's always good to check when you're back!' said Jayojit, and drank the water urgently. 'You know one could get dehydrated sitting on a plane for so long!' he said, putting down the glass. 'These old glasses,' he murmured, looking at the glass quizzically.

Vikram drank some of the water slowly and then stopped as

if he could drink no more, and his grandmother said, 'Enough, shona?' The boy nodded seriously and gave her the glass, which she accepted as if it were a gift, with a smile.

'But tell me, Joy,' said his father, visibly irked and hot, 'what made you take Bangladesh Biman of all airlines? Surely there are other, better airlines coming from America? I can't believe that the best option is coming with all those Bangladeshis all the way from New York!'

'Baba,' said Jayojit, 'the truth is there are a lot of airlines coming to Calcutta, all of them from third-rate East European countries—Rumanian, Yugoslav, Aeroflot of the defunct Soviet Union. KLM, Thai—I couldn't get seats. Air India—if I *have* to tolerate rudeness, I'd rather it wasn't from air hostesses who've got their jobs because of some reservation quota. At least in Bangladesh Biman, which doesn't follow a *single* international regulation and isn't even a member of the IATA, you have all these placid East Bengalis all around you, speaking to each other in dialect. Baba, I realized, sitting on that plane, why Bangladesh is the way it is: they're all *happy*, and their marriages are working! Look at what happened to the Hindus who left.' His own parents were of East Bengali origin, the father coming from a landowning family in Chittagong, the mother from Mymensingh. Apparently a few distant relatives had stayed on in the ancestral houses; a small businessman, a teacher—they were rarely in touch with them. 'Besides, baba,' chuckled Jayojit, 'the tickets are less expensive.'

'They're certainly less expensive from here!' agreed the father, looking very concerned behind the beard, but in a way that suggested he was enjoying himself. 'Every week tens of middle-class Bengalis who've been saving up all their lives queue up in the airport to travel by Bangladesh Biman—to visit their son or daughter in England, or to travel: you know the Bengali weakness for "bhraman"? Last week your Ranjit mesho and Dolly mashi, you remember them'—he looked reflective—'took a Biman flight to London.' The light glinted on his spectacles.

Jayojit pictured the couple in the check-in section of Calcutta airport, with its minuscule international air traffic and the rude officials behind the counters, Ranjit mesho and Dolly mashi, confused but not unhappy, with their suitcases, he looking like what he was, an executive whose career had begun well but not taken off, but who still believed in the system, happy to be going abroad, no matter that it was by Bangladesh Biman, and Dolly mashi, always in a printed sari, saving her good saris for who knows which day, accompanied by the same two suitcases they must always use when travelling.

'And the tickets are affordable—21,000 rupees,' said the Admiral in a strangely hurt way. 'If you can tolerate Dhaka!' No reference was made to the fact that they had planned themselves to travel by Biman to America before the divorce had taken place; the unspoken reference to that possibility hung in the air like something that did not need to be said.

'How are their children, that reminds me?' asked Jayojit, pursuing a normal conversation. 'Indra and what's her name?'

'Oh, they're all right,' said his father, a little disgusted, as if they couldn't possibly be anything but 'all right'. 'One in England

and one in America … Indra is a scientist.'

'Always thought he would be.'

Vikram was in the balcony, looking at the potted plants which were placed half in sunlight and half in shadow; geometric shadows from the grille fell on the wall and the floor, giving a kind of visual relief; in his hand he held a small unfinished carton of pure orange juice he had taken out of his rucksack, whose dregs he sipped contentedly through a bent plastic straw whenever he stood still.

'But Bonny liked the Bangladesh Biman chicken curry!' said Jayojit. 'Didn't you, Bonny?'

The boy turned to look back, in surprise. Then, as if the words had reached him an instant late, he nodded.

Now Jayojit's mother emerged again and said to Vikram:

'Come on, we are going to have nice Bengali fish for lunch. So let us have bath now.'

'All right, tamma,' said the boy, stepping out of the shade of the verandah into the drawing room.

He was her elder son's only child—her only grandchild, born seven years ago. Last year he had written her a letter beginning, 'Dear thamma …', and it should have been an occasion for great pleasure, and it was, but that night she had lain thinking of what was happening, and the reasons why, and she had cried.

His blue t-shirt, which looked soiled and tired, and darkened at the sides, he took off and laid on the bed; divested of it, he looked surprisingly fresh, his upper body pale, he erect and ready for the bath as his grandmother took him into the bathroom. Barefoot now, he seemed to be enjoying walking on the cool floor of the flat, his toes curled a little at the thrill of the coolness.

'Come—I will bathe you,' said his grandmother, tying the aanchal of her sari around herself.

'No!' said the boy, in a voice that was small but clear. Shyly, he added, 'Just show me how to work the shower.'

Although she felt a great urge to wash him, she restrained herself, for she sensed around him a wall of privacy he had grown up with—no fault of his, he was not even aware of it—which Jayojit did not have.

'Last time I bathed you—you remember?' she said. 'We had so much fun!'

She advanced a few steps to the lever on the wall with the hot and cold water knobs on either side, which to the boy probably looked antiquated, and she said:

'I turn it like—*this*—and then I turn on the water like *this!*' She was standing to the right, her left arm straining as she turned the knobs, and her two bangles, her iron wedding-bangle and a gold one, clashed against each other.

'Wooo!' said the boy as it rained on him, and he burst out laughing, a long series of delighted giggles. His grandmother, standing just outside the shower area, looked at him and smiled. His eyes and face were shut tightly. His arm reached out for the crevice in the wall where the soap was placed, and his hand closed around a new, waxy bar of Lux.

'I have kept clean towel for you, Bonny,' called out his grandmother, as if he were further away than he really was.

10

He nodded vigorously, spitting out water, his hair plastered to his skull, his eyes still closed. 'I'm going now,' she called again, and this time he did not respond. He had begun to play, quite independently, with the hot and cold water taps, adjusting them with his small hands. He hardly required any hot water; in April, the tanks became so hot that warm water flowed out of the cold water taps.

Later, as Bonny was drying himself, and investigating a scab on his elbow which had begun to itch, Jayojit came into the room; the conversation—the 'adda'—outside between father and son had temporarily come to an end; both had had to tear themselves away; how Jayojit thirsted, without knowing it, for the pleasures of adda when he was in America! 'I'll be back to continue this conversation from where we left off,' he warned his father as he rose from his chair; now he sat on the bed, untying his shoelaces with a look of great satisfaction, as if it were the climax to his journey, ready to go in for a bath himself.

'Had a shower, Bonny?' he said.

'Uh-huh,' said the boy. 'Baba, I don't have any clothes,' he added, the towel covering his head like a hood.

'All right,' said Jayojit, with the air of one who is familiar with and used to such situations, 'we'll take your clothes out right now,' and he bent down on his knees to unlock the suitcase, and retrieved a new t-shirt from an apparently prodigious store of folded t-shirts, and a pair of shorts, and laid them carefully on the bed. The boy stared interestedly at his clothes.

In the kitchen, Jayojit's mother was setting pieces of rui fish afloat in burning oil.

His mother was not the best possible cook, and these days she had a helper who did some of the cooking in the morning; this helper was not a very good cook either. But Jayojit was not too fussy about food and nor was the Admiral; for the latter, especially, home food was just a routine, and had to be healthy and cooked in a small amount of oil; excesses in connection with food were to be indulged in at the club Christmas or New Year's Eve parties, where strangely shaped gateaux were served, and people queued up for their portion of barbecued steak and sautéed vegetables.

Home food was safe and insipid, and had a tranquillity about it; today there was a watery lentil daal in a chinaware bowl, fried rui, a dalna which was a combination of sweet gourd and cabbage leaves among other things, and a preparation of pabdaa fish in mustard. It was an honest, even joyful, effort by his mother, though it had not quite worked; but it was not wholly tasteless either.

'The pabdaa is very fresh,' said Jayojit appreciatively. He was eating with his fingers.

His father, bent and serious, now and then dabbing his white beard with a napkin, was eating silently. He was old-fashioned; he rarely praised his wife's cooking, but kept his ears pricked, like a child's, for others' praises. More and more his wife had become to him like a mother and a nurse, giving him his medicine with a glass of water, serving his food, to which he submitted with a helpless, sour-faced, child-like decorum, and overlooking, with good humour, his constant need to exercise his inconsequential tyrannical hold over this household, in which usually only he and his wife lived, with part-time servants coming and going each day. He ate with a fork and a spoon as he always did, laboriously, as if haunted by the expectation or memory of some pain—perhaps the mild stroke he had had seven years ago, which any day might recur. Above them, the fan with its three blades turned swiftly, generously, but invisibly, distributing air. Bonny sat next to his grandfather, perky after the bath; he had had nothing but daal and rice and a piece of the fried rui.

'The daal's good,' he said, holding up his spoon.

'Have the other fish, shona,' said his grandmother. 'Try the vegetables.'

'Let him have the daal, ma,' said Jayojit. 'Just thank your stars he's eating something!'

The boy stopped eating, the food still in his mouth, and looked around guiltily, but also pleased at this exchange about him, and at this description of himself as someone difficult and intractable; he was interested in his father's portrait of himself.

Now the Admiral, having deftly divested the fish of its flesh with his fork and spoon, leaving only the bones, picked up the pabdaa head with his spoon, intending to chew it; the sound of his breathing surrounded him.

'Is dadu going to eat the head of that fish, baba?' asked the boy in concern.

'Dadu likes fish-head,' said Jayojit loudly, as if everything he said were important.

'Can I have a look at it?'

'Certainly,' said his grandfather. 'Have a good look at it.'

So the boy stood up and peered at his grandfather's plate, at the long pabdaa bone, and the fish-head with its eyes lying on the spoon.

'All right?' said the grandfather.

The boy nodded seriously and sat down again, and began to finish what was left of his daal and rice.

In the afternoon, when the meal was over, Jayojit's father sat on a chair for some time; he was not supposed to lie down immediately after eating. His wife brought him pills which he swallowed noisily with a glass of water.

Now, in the afternoon heat before siesta, they seemed to feel the incompleteness of their family, and that it would not be now complete. Someone was missing. Both mother and father were too hurt to speak of it. In a strange way, they felt abandoned.

'Won't you rest?' asked the Admiral after a while. 'I think I'll go and lie down,' he said.

'You do that, baba,' said Jayojit, getting up himself. Vikram was playing with two toy dinosaurs in the corridor; his father passed him on the way to the room.

Inside the room, Jayojit began to unpack the suitcase. He did not want to sleep; if he slept now, he would be asleep till midnight. So he began to hang up his shirts and trousers in the cupboard, and put handkerchiefs, vests, and underwear in the drawers; Bonny's things went into the drawers as well. He was not as familiar with the house as he should be; his parents had moved here eight years ago, and he had visited only three times since then. His own feelings towards the flat were thus partially ones of familiarity and trust, and partially a complex of other feelings—of amusement and amazement at the mass-produced design, of both pity and avuncular, affection for its bathrooms, tiles, furniture, verandah, and a basic admiration for, and acceptance of, its reliability. He realized that neither his mother nor father could see any of these things, and thus he too could not see them separately from the flat they had made their own.

One by one, he hung his shirts from the hanger, where they took on, inside the cupboard, a fleeting resemblance to his proportions. A sense of potential being, simple but true, now inhabited the cupboard. Some of the shelves were covered with newspaper; peering at them while arranging the clothes, Jayojit furrowed his eyebrows and snorted humorously. Something about Marxism and liberalization: the paper couldn't be very old. The hard-core Marxists and trade unions wanted to know how the Chief Minister would reconcile liberalization with Marxist beliefs; Basu had offered China as an example. Then the paper was covered with clothes.

Next, he unzipped the shoulder bag and retrieved his shaving things and his and Vikram's toilet accessories, Aquafresh toothpaste, Head and Shoulders shampoo, Bodyline deodorant, a cylinder of Old Spice shaving foam, a Backwood Insect Cutter which he'd bought in case of mosquitoes; these things gleamed the most and looked the most foreign and desirable; even the toothbrushes were different and, curving oddly, seemed to belong to the future and some fragile, opulent culture. Jayojit kept padding off, barefoot, with an intent air, to the bathroom, and placing them on the small ledge of glass above the basin.

By half-past three, it was not so much the boy but the dinosaurs that had become exhausted; two small blue and pink creatures that had once ruled the world, they lay now on their sides upon the floor, their tails still curving, their heads bent and mouths open to roar, but strangely frozen and dumb. They were so small they could hardly be seen. Vikram sat upon an armchair, concentrating upon a storybook, turning the pages and looking at the pictures.

Later, the doorbell rang, and Jayojit's mother could be heard opening the door and saying, 'So late?' A maid-servant came in; she was trying hard to hide her guilty look, and went quickly to the kitchen to wash the dishes.

'Where do you get them from?' asked Jayojit. She really looked as if she'd come straight from the village.

'They sit downstairs and work in the flats in the building,' said Jayojit's mother. 'If you dismiss one it's difficult to get another, because they're all friends.'

'Oh, so it's a trade union!' said Jayojit cheerfully.

'Trade union, nonsense!' said Jayojit's mother. 'They're just a bunch of shirkers who pretend to be friendly with each other.'

By evening Bonny had begun to feel sleepy. At half-past

seven he fell asleep on the sofa without, to his grandmother's disappointment, having had dinner.

'It's all right, ma,' said Jayojit, who had changed into a pink sleeping suit that looked ridiculous on his large frame; he went about barefoot in the kitchen getting himself a bottle of water for the night. Bonny was still in his shorts, but his father did not wake him; when he picked him up in his arms to put him into bed the boy mumbled something, and he said, 'All right, baba, all right, Bonny.'

The boy knitted his eyebrows, turned his mouth, and sniffed, as if he could smell something. There was probably nothing more peaceful for him than these moments of subconscious awareness, suspended in his father's arms, between two places of rest. Jayojit laid him on the bed. It was a two-bedroom flat, and theirs was the smaller room, but it had an air-conditioner in it: a luxury.

Ever since evening, the sound of television music and the voices of television characters had begun to come from the other flats, like a form of public dreaming. But when Jayojit turned on the air-conditioner, nothing could be heard but its hum.

The Admiral had a car, an old Fiat, but did not use it often. And he did not have a driver. Costs were too high these days; the cost of petrol, drivers' salaries, things in general. The last driver was a man called Alam, a tired-looking man who'd slept his way through most of his employment.

The Admiral was always aggressively telling his wife to save, though she still found it difficult to adjust to the different rhythms of expenditure required after retirement. For a while he had been engaged as a consultant in a Marwari company, and then given it up; he had grown fed up going to the office daily for what he thought a paltry salary, and having to put up with what he discovered, after the navy, was a rather peculiar style of functioning. The next year he'd got rid of the driver and never employed one since; anyway, they all spoilt the car with their tinkering. When he'd been Admiral, stationed first in Cochin (in the Southern Naval Command; he'd retired as Rear-Admiral, in spite of being known to everyone as, in short, 'Admiral') and then in Delhi, it had been a dream-world; everything had been done for them; they'd had a huge bungalow wherever they went, a car, coloured the navy's deep blue (to denote the sea) with two stars painted on the back—identifying his rank—and they'd never thought the value of money would depreciate so rapidly after retirement—they'd never thought of the value of money before. If you were unemployed or had retired, the Admiral said, it was better not to be in India but somewhere else. The institution, even the country, you had served did nothing for you; they gave you everything as long as you were working, but in old age you had to manage your life and your finances yourself.

A major drain on their savings had been the Admiral's stroke; doctors, medicines, the hospital—the expensive business of keeping oneself alive. Of course, the government had contributed to hospitalization costs, but they could not be genuinely concerned—the Admiral's health was only an abstraction to them. His principal preoccupations now concerned his savings, and that Jayojit should start afresh, or, after what had happened, at least lead the second half of his life decently. He thought about these matters every day.

He now stood at the bus stop on the main road, dressed in his favourite attire, white bush shirt and white trousers and strapped sandals. These clothes kept him cool in the heat. He was going to take a bus to the bank, where he had some enquiries to make about an investment bond.

Jayojit had woken up late, at eleven. He had had a bath, and then changed into a shirt and shorts. Wearing shorts exposed his large fair thighs and calves, covered with smooth strands of black hair. His mother seemed to notice nothing unusual about his clothes; parents accept that offspring who live abroad will appear to them in a slightly altered incarnation, and are even disappointed if they do not. As he came out of his room, in which the air-conditioner had run all night, he encountered a blast of hot air—the normal temperature at this time in the house.

'Ma!' he said. 'Anything to eat?'

It was not that he was particularly hungry; and he had still not been to the toilet; his body seemed to be functioning to another time, or not properly to this one; but he had experienced this dislocation before and could ignore it. It was the previous night now in America; already America had become dream-like. He had heard sounds of frying in the kitchen, and found his mother inside standing before the cooker, and Bonny loitering beside her; he did not seem in the least troubled by jet-lag, but seemed to have been remade and reshaped by this new climate, standing there watching his grandmother.

'I'm making luchis,' said Jayojit's mother, without turning around from the kodai before her. 'Bonny shona has already had one with sugarcane gur—I melted it.'

'Baba,' said the boy, 'it tastes just like maple syrup!'

'Have you brushed your teeth?' asked Jayojit.

'He's done everything,' said his mother in Bengali. 'He came out of the room at eight o'clock in the morning, and I took him inside again and he brushed his teeth. Then I took out his half-pants and vest and a new shirt from the drawer—you were fast asleep—and I brought him to my bathroom, where he had a bath. Isn't that right, Bonny?'

Bonny, who had been staring mutely at his grandmother, as if he were lip-reading, nodded. He could follow the language—he had so often heard his mother and father talk in it in his first five years—but he could not speak it. It was both a disadvantage and an odd privilege that set him apart, and caused others around him here to make that small extra effort to communicate themselves to him.

'Then, some time ago, Bonny said you had woken up and gone to take a bath, and I began to fry the luchis.'

'Well, gur is not maple syrup,' said Jayojit to his son. He added, explanatorily, and with an inflection of pride, 'He loves maple syrup.'

Earlier in the morning, a temporary help had come and cooked a dry vegetable preparation. This was waiting outside on the dining table in a covered porcelain bowl, slivers of pumpkin and potatoes fried with onions and black jeera. It had become pleasantly cool with the passing of time, and went well with the hot luchis, and contrasted temperately with the general heat. Jayojit sat on a chair and broke the luchis and ate, a giant in his shorts, one large leg crossed over another.

'I mustn't eat too much, though,' he said. 'I'm putting on weight.'

Ever since he had become single again he had begun to eat what he could in America, indiscriminately plundering the shelves in the supermarket for frozen food and pizzas. He had first read about TV dinners in *Mad* magazine when he was growing up: what glamour pizzas had, then! These days, in America, he looked at food, as he did many other things, emotionlessly, as something that could be put to use and cooked quickly.

'Where—I don't think you have put on weight,' protested his mother, returning from the kitchen with a cup of tea.

She could not know of his secret life in that continent, of driving down the motorway, going to the supermarket, filling up a trolley with things, his orphanhood and distance from his country and parents, and that of other people like him, wandering around the aisles of the supermarket in shorts, with wives, or perhaps alone, with the ex-wife somewhere completely else, running into each other and saying, 'How are you? Still around?' His mother could not even imagine it. There was a South Indian couple, the Nairs, he had run into three times at the supermarket he shopped at. They had had an arranged marriage (he had gone back to India to marry her); he was dark, pleasantly blunt-nosed, bespectacled, and had a moustache; she was curly-haired, large-eyed, and dark. Nair had a degree in biochemistry, and worked as a marketing man in a phar-maceutical company. They had met only once socially; but, in the vegetable section of the supermarket, they had discovered each other with surprised exclamations again and again. He had learnt that, unsurprisingly, they were vegetarians. The first time they had met at the lunch party, Jayojit had been with his wife Amala; but, at the supermarket, he was already alone, and they, after the first occasion, had not asked about her: word got around so quickly among the network of Indians they would have known. Jayojit enjoyed Nair's South Indian accent, its slow intimacy, and his wife wore slacks and a loose t-shirt and a large bindi on her forehead.

'And what did you do all morning?' said Jayojit to Bonny.

'He has been playing with his Jurassic Park rakkhosh,' said the boy's grandmother. 'All morning … They were lying on the floor last night and I put them on the table. This morning, he showed them to his dadu.'

'You scared of them, tamma?' asked the boy.

'Naturally I am! They are two rakkhosh!'

'Tamma knows *about* Jurassic Park, but she hasn't *seen* it,' explained Bonny to his father. 'It came to Calcutta two months ago, baba. Isn't that neat?'

There had, in fact, been great excitement in the city with the coming of the film; crowds of people outside Nandan cinema.

'Ma,' said Jayojit, looking up suddenly, 'can I have a glass of water?'

'Of course, baba,' she said, rising. 'I'll bring it right now.'

This made him remember that his father had never called him 'baba' as many Bengali fathers do their sons the age-old, loving, inexplicable practice of fathers calling their sons 'father'—but always called him Jayojit, and nothing else; bringing an element of formality into their relationship, and also, he supposed, a note of respect for him. But, on the other hand, Jayojit had remarked silently that he sometimes called Bonny 'dadu', as if he were allowing himself to be more paternal, more Bengali, with his grandson; perhaps, with Bonny's birth, he had begun a new phase in his life—who can tell the exact changes that take place in people, which are possibly unknown to themselves? Till they die, people keep trying to innocently adjust to life.

Jayojit's mother returned with a glass of water, a tumbler from the old set they used to get free from the Services. He drank the refrigerated water, which had caused a dew of condensation to form on the glass, gratefully.

'Aah,' he said, wiping his mouth. 'Tea is all right, but it makes one feel hot in this climate. What one needs is gallons of cold water!'

His mother smiled.

'Where's baba?' he asked.

'He's gone to the bank, to settle some matters,' she said, and Jayojit recognized, with an inward smile, a touching and naive piousness in her tone, as if she were speaking of some mysterious but trusted god who knew his business no matter if he were a god who had almost died of a stroke seven years ago.

'In this heat?' asked Jayojit. 'Is that good for him?'

'He always goes to the bank once a week,' his mother said, again with that piousness that could not understand criticism. 'He takes the bus.'

'Is that necessary?' asked Jayojit, genuinely concerned. 'How are you financially?'

'God alone knows, these things I don't understand,' she said reticently. 'You must ask your baba.'

Bonny had gone off to one side of the sitting room, and was playing between the armchairs and the sofa. There was no real difference between the sitting and dining room; they were part of the same hall, and only an imaginary partition existed between the two. The architect had thrown the dining space on the side of the kitchen and the small corridor to the front door, a pleasant limbo or island with its dining table and chairs; while the hall was pushed into the interior, and was adjoined to the semi-outdoors of the verandah. Here, not far away from his father and grandmother, and fully in their sights, Bonny had become transformed into another being, making noises with his mouth and throat, indicating the propulsion and motion of some agent of locomotion—perhaps an aeroplane. As he wandered among the furniture, he imitated moments of vertigo and others of equilibrium and rest.

'Well, I'd better get up now,' Jayojit said. 'There are things to do.'

He had begun to feel the first movements in his bowels, and was oddly grateful and relieved; he was always lost when jet-lag caused his body to skip its more basic functionings.

'Have another luchi, Joy!' said his mother. She picked up one from the last droopy ones that hadn't puffed up properly. 'There are many more.'

'Ha ha … No, ma—there's a limit to the luchis you can digest,' said Jayojit. Before he went into his room, he said, 'Be careful, Bonny!'

The Admiral returned at half-past eleven, ringing the doorbell three times. When he came in, his beard was untidy and parts of his white shirt were dark with sweat and clung to his skin.

'Damn bank!' he said, walking towards his right to the bedroom. 'Can't make the scoundrels work—it's these damn unions!'

He went inside the room without addressing his wife directly—he never spoke to her unless he had to—and, having put the papers inside, came out again after a minute. Still in his sweat-stained shirt, he switched on the fan and sat on the sofa in the sitting room with a newspaper.

'Is it *really* hot outside?' asked Bonny, standing by his grandfather's right arm and waiting for an answer.

'Hot and dusty, dadu,' said his grandfather between breaths. 'Hot and dusty.' He was still breathing hard, as if his heart were pumping and exercising in a way that it would if he were getting off a bus or still walking down the road.

He was a large man of medium height, and was overweight; though he hid his bulk from himself and others by wearing loose white bush shirts, it could nevertheless be seen, especially now when the shirt stuck to parts of him and revealed the heaviness of his contours. He was not uncomfortable with his body; it was part of his presence. Although doctors had told him to lose weight, he forgot their advice the moment they were out of earshot.

'Baba—you're back!' said Jayojit, coming out of the room and padding toward his father in his rubber sandals. He looked large and cool. 'How did it go?'

'It's a miracle these banks work, and that any money flows through this state!' said the Admiral. 'Everyone belongs to a trade union, and no one believes in service. You ask them a question, and they're busy talking to each other about a cricket match or a relative's wedding!' Used to being deferred to at home and at work, he had realized in his post-retirement years in Calcutta that his commanding presence was of no use at post offices and banks; in fact, the clerks seemed to sense he took his privileges for granted and resented it. At these places, he had to learn to tone down his voice, to wait patiently like everyone else in silence.

'Which bank do you use? Grindlays?' asked Jayojit.

'I had work at the State Bank today.'

'State Bank? Why on earth d'you use the State Bank?'

'They've started a new investment scheme, actually,' said the Admiral. 'However,' he laughed grimly, 'most people in the bank don't even seem to know about it! I had to ask to see the manager—he gave me some papers. They'd even advertised it today.' He shook the *Statesman*, in wonder and contempt.

'What about share prices?' asked Jayojit. 'The share market is doing well, isn't it—new companies coming in?' The Admiral shook his head. 'My savings are mainly in government bonds. I have hardly anything in shares,' he said. 'I don't know enough about them.'

Jayojit nodded. Although he was an economist, he knew more about economic theory than shrewd investment, about global trends and third-world markets, but as to how they intersected with something particular and real, like his father's personal life and decisions—that was different, and beyond the scope of his discipline.

'Why don't you ask Haru kaku?' said Jayojit, thinking of a cousin of his father's, a chartered accountant.

'Haru!' said his father, as if the name had startled him. 'Haru's long retired. Besides, I don't believe everything he says.'

In principle, Jayojit was all for this new flood—of investors and companies coming into the country. During the time of the Rajiv Gandhi government, when the Prime Minister had been gathering advisors around himself, mainly from among his Cambridge friends, someone had recommended Jayojit, who was then teaching at Buffalo. Jayojit had sent him a plan, suggesting gradual liberalization; thus, he had been there, in a sense, at the beginning. In the new, as yet unfinished, brickwork of India's new economic order, Jayojit had laid an early and important cornerstone. Nothing but economic reform, he believed, could change India from a country living on borrowings from the West into a productive and competitive one. Yet now, when he saw his father's hesitation about investing in shares, for which he had neither the means nor the confidence, he had no advice to give him.

In the afternoon, the Admiral lay in his trousers and shirt on the bed, his head against two pillows, and slept. He snored, and then the snores dissolved once more into regular heavy breathing.

At about three o'clock someone rang the doorbell and Jayojit's mother went to open the door. It was the maidservant; there was an exchange at the door in low voices, and the maid, eyes downcast, came into the flat. She went straight to the kitchen.

Apparently she was supposed to come once in the morning, to clean the floors, and once in the afternoon to wash the dishes. But she had failed to turn up this morning. Her explanation was that the Mitras, whose flat she worked in—she worked part-time in four flats in the building each day—hadn't let her go.

'Their washerwoman didn't come today, ma!' she protested.

Jayojit's mother was certain she had been chattering downstairs with her friends. 'Always acting the innocent,' she muttered. Her name was Maya—Jayojit had overheard his mother call her this.

Out she came now from the kitchen, and began to lightly dust the furniture. Then she stooped to pick up, in an unenquiring, unsurprised way, the small cars and vehicles, trailers, trucks, which Bonny had left on the floor; she put them on a side table. After sweeping the floor she closed the front door and left as quietly as she had come.

It was simple—Jayojit wanted to spend as much time as possible with him. Although it was clear that he and his wife hadn't got on from the very beginning, some urge to rehearse what their parents had done before them had taken hold of him, of her, and, without fully understanding what they were doing, they had brought a child into the world, in a small nursing home in a midwestern American town.

Bonny had been born three years after the marriage. The first two years were the years of amorous energy. Yet it had been absurd. Both Amala and Jayojit had grown up with the same background, listened to the same music, liked the Beatles; she, predictably, shied away from the Rolling Stones as so many girls he used to know in school had. He had clung to the loyalties he thought he was shaped by; she had seamlessly allowed herself to shed her early enthusiasms, which probably hadn't been very intense in the first place, and, listening to the incomprehensible music of the eighties, would say, 'What's wrong with it?' At first, he found this touching. Both of them had decided, at some point in their lives, without articulating it to themselves, like a pact they'd made with several others without knowing it, that an arranged marriage was the best option.

Bonny now went to a school in San Diego, near where his mother lived. He was at that stage when only the simplest arithmetic—addition, subtraction, multiplication—was taught, when five-sentence compositions were assigned to be written. Jayojit had to meet the head teacher to request from the school an extra month off for Bonny's holidays. 'I don't think it should be a problem, Dr Chatterjee.' The lady knew he taught at a college. 'Vikram's bright; he should pick things up as easily at home as he does at school. You know, I envy you your trip. The furthest I've been into Asia is Paris.'

Jayojit had laughed on cue. Then, suddenly, curious for knowledge, he'd asked:

'How's he doing? Anything in particular he's good at … or weak in, for that matter?'

He cherished the notion of his child's success, although, in his own life, he'd come to disdain conventional ideas of success and achievement.

'He's good at English, I'd say. I teach them English.'

'Oh, really?'

'Yes.' Did she seem disappointed that Bonny hadn't told him already? 'He's quite good. Other children have problems with little things like distinguishing between its and it apostrophe s, and constructions like "had had", but a few, like Bonny, don't. He's also good at making sentences and spelling.'

He began to go out for walks with Bonny in the afternoon.

The Admiral said, 'Does dadu have homework to do? I could help him.'

'Not really, baba. He's too young for homework; he has to do some drawings and listen to some stories, that's all. Last month he wrote a two-sentence story about going to the beach.' He laughed. The Admiral listened gravely, as if to the description of a thesis. 'Listen: "The beach is full of sand and it sure gets hot. Mary went out to the sea and got afraid."' Jayojit had it by heart. 'That apparently got an alpha.' Feigning surprise.

At times, in his old school, Bonny'd have to self-consciously play the 'Indian' role when nations were being discussed, and he'd been told by his father: 'Hey, d'you know what Vikram means: it means strong, powerful, heroic.'

'Really?' Bonny had said. 'That's weird.'

As they went out now they could hear voices coming from some of the other flats, where housewives were watching videos as their children slept. The noise of fights and crescendos took Jayojit aback at first.

Sometimes they did not take the lift and went down the stairs; Bonny, in particular, liked running down. Bits of garbage would be lying here and there on each landing.

When they had arrived downstairs, they were met by a hall. The hall was usually swept by breezes, especially now, in April. At one end, on the far right, there was a row of wooden post-boxes with numbers painted on them, where a postman could be seen sometimes at half-past four, and near the centre of the hall there was a ping-pong table.

'It's amazing the time at which these men come,' Jayojit had thought as he'd watched, three days ago, a man arrived with a bag of letters at four o' clock. 'But if you tell them anything, they won't give your mail tomorrow.'

There were terrible stories about the post-office, how registered letters lay waiting, and how overseas mail, with blue stickers saying Par Avion, was delivered weeks late. 'It's worse than inconvenient, it can be downright fatal,' someone had said. Even phone bills didn't come on time. Each time Jayojit wrote to his parents from America he felt a renewed sense of irritation and helplessness.

'Baba!' said Bonny urgently, pausing in the centre of the hall. Jayojit, preoccupied, stood there seeming to watch him, although his mind was elsewhere. He did not know how to think of these first days together of their visit, if 'visit' it could be called.

As they crossed the hall and descended the four steps into the compound, they came out into the heat. The two or three maidservants who loitered here weren't there. Before Jayojit and Bonny was a sort of lawn or garden with railings on all sides. There were trees in it—two palm trees which seemed to have taken refuge here from a more exotic habitat, a mango tree—and flowering shrubs and even clone-like potted plants. Late in the morning, once or twice, Jayojit had woken up from jet-lag at dawn to see the mali alone among the pots, unwittingly scaring birds away, watering the plants.

By the gates, a cat, curled up in the heat, looked warily at Bonny without raising its head; Bonny returned its gaze frankly.

On the other side of the gate, a young watchman on his bench, whose moustache was so tender and dark that he might never have shaved it, watched the boy and his father, the combination of trousers, shorts, and sneakers.

'Where's dadu and tamma?' asked Bonny, squinting upward, as if a vague memory had nudged him after a long time. He scratched his scalp where it had begun to perspire slightly.

But dadu and thamma must be asleep.

'They're on that side,' said his father, a bright star of light reflecting off his spectacles. 'You can't see them from here.' They both looked up at the apartment block facing them, with its numerous verandahs.

'We don't live on this side, baba?' asked Bonny, disappointed for no reason.

'No, we don't, Bonny,' said Jayojit. 'If we did, we'd see this garden from our balcony, wouldn't we?'

'I guess.' This was acquiesced world-wearily.

The watchman was still looking at the two; not meaning to be rude; indeed, his face was like a door that was open, friendly, unguarded. On closer observation, it was evident that he was staring at them without seeing them. It was as if he—a young man of about twenty-one—were asleep with his eyes open; at least until he stirred a little. He hadn't seen them before, but this was not unusual; tenants were always coming and going from the building, as were owners of flats or members of their family. Bonny, for instance, had been here only twice in the last three years, and each time he'd been a different shape; really, a different person. And it was not difficult to tell when people had arrived from abroad; something about their clothes, and the way they spoke with each other, the way they appeared, transforming the life of whichever family they were visiting, and then vanished again, tipping the maidservant extravagantly.

The watchman was looking at the way Jayojit was standing and talking to his son. A servant passed by and then a car hesitated by the gate; the watchman got up, distracted, like a traveller in a departure lounge who realizes, after an unspecified interval, that his name's being announced.

This space between the steps into the building and the main gates to the lane was where the sun beat down intensely. But clouds would be conjured up in the sky from nothing. On their second afternoon out, one or two big drops had dashed against the ground, becoming dark spots where they'd fallen on the driveway.

As they were looking up at the building, a dog in one of the first-floor balconies began to bark. It was an Alsatian; it seemed furious at being confined inside the flat.

'It's a dog, baba,' Bonny informed his father.

Jayojit, tall, one part of him comparing this heat to the drier heat of the American South, wondered why people who lived in flats hardly big enough for a medium-sized family should keep dogs. This dog barked to the shadows in the outside world from the eternal but cluttered present of the balcony, amidst pots, a clothesline, and two plastic chairs like dwarves in the background.

'Hi!' The small voice was drowned by a fresh fit of loud barking.

'It's a nice-looking dog, Bonny, but it doesn't seem to be in a very good mood.'

There was a gulmohar tree in the lane, the flaming orange flowers erupting from within, and banyan trees, private and removed as ancient pilgrims. Some drivers were asleep inside Ambassadors; others were crowded together outside, handkerchiefs spread, playing cards. Near the gates, in the blue shadow not of the building but of a wall behind, there were two ramshackle structures: a tea stall, which catered, with thick slices of bread and biscuits, to the drivers, and a dhobi's shop, where clothes from the building were ironed.

When Jayojit couldn't sleep the first few nights, he'd reread the morning's *Statesman,* the headlines become strange at the end of the day, when the appositeness that news had in the morning—calamities and predictions—had already passed into its daily afterlife.

There was one he'd been fooled by, an advertisement pretending to be a report, with the headline 'Miraculous Antidote to Hair Loss Announced', which he began to read with the same unquestioning acceptance with which he read the rest of the newspaper, before he came to its end and realized what it was. It began: 'It was announced today that finally ...' and had just the right mixture of breathlessness and objectivity. Very clever, thought Jayojit. After this, he folded the paper, switched off the lamp, and tried to sleep.

Waking at home, in his house in Claremont, used to be

difficult, with Bonny gone, withheld from him like a promise, and Amala, his wife, gone. Some of the pictures she had bought— prints; pichwais with serene trains of elephants, the cowherd-god, dallying with the gopis, identified by the peacock-plume above the forehead—were still on the walls. Mornings were quiet in Claremont; it was as if they waited till radio alarm clocks began to play and people got up. He lay still before he rose in his house in Claremont, feeling quite separate from the man who'd written a book about economic development, who drove a Ford, who'd secured tenure.

The luchis continued to appear. If his mother had lived in the nineteenth century, she, in spite of her pale complexion and occasional fatigued look, would have been happiest and busiest in the kitchen; alone and happy, not involved in the changes disturbing history and coming over others', anonymous lives.

'Ma, this has got to stop!'

'Joy, you will not get luchis over there.'

His mother had fixed ideas about what his life 'over there' was like. She had never been abroad; it was an imaginary place for her, a territory that intersected with her life without ever actually touching it, and which had, for her, its own recognizable characteristics. Two years ago, she might have gone there for the first time, if they hadn't had to abandon their trip quite abruptly. Now her bangles shook as she put two luchis on Jayojit's plate. Bonny, sitting next to Jayojit, was having milk and cornflakes. His father was having, as he did from whenever it was Jayojit's memory could stretch back to, a soft-boiled egg and dry toast. That toast had been subject to vicissitude, once it was lightly buttered, and sometimes covered with a skin of Kissan marmalade, freckled with orange rind; this had been the taste of breakfast, in war and in peace.

'But, baba,' Bonny said very gravely, 'you can have cornflakes if you don't want *lu-chis*.'

From ten o'clock to eleven, for the first ten days or so, Jayojit lay down full-length upon the sofa, his legs arched slightly, his hands holding the newspaper over almost one half of his body. In front of Jayojit's reclining figure, in the verandah, had appeared a new set of clothes drying on the clothesline—Bonny's and his—almost crisp with the heat from the morning, hanging indecisively.

'But you must not take out the little boy'—*'bachcha chhele'* was how she referred to her grandson—'in the sun. How will he take it? And suddenly if he falls ill?' said Jayojit's mother, agitated and having lapsed, without warning, into a worked-upness.

Jayojit dismissed this cursorily, his eyes still upon newsprint, eking out the fantasy of a holiday and saying casually to his mother:

'Oh, he'll be OK, ma. Don't fuss. He's tough.'

Bonny overheard this with the air of a passer-by whose route had intersected, briefly, the conversation of strangers. He had gone, as usual, to the verandah, where his own blue drying shirt dangled over him indeterminately.

'Okay,' managed Jayojit after ten minutes, as if he'd drifted into a coma in the meanwhile. 'Okay. You have a point. I'll take care he doesn't get too much exposure.'

Someone was not present, and part of the conversation, of the concern, was directed at that absent figure, or at least took her into account. She—Jayojit's ex-wife; Bonny's mother—was more and more real in her separate, everyday existence. Yet Bonny's grandmother was too full of her own worry, her bosom working with affection, to think of this. She gazed at Bonny with the intensity of one who hadn't seen him enough.

Sometimes, in the afternoon, Jayojit came out and stood in the corridor outside the flat, taking in the breeze. He wasn't wholly comfortable; a door stared at him from the left-hand corner. Yet the flat was hotter than it should be, because it faced the west, while the corridor received the breeze coming from the south-east.

'That's better,' said Jayojit. From here he got a partial view of the back of the building. Facing him were the many windows and verandahs at the rear of the flats, the dark, recurring backs of air-conditioners protruding outward; and, when he turned his head to the left, he could see part of a cricket field that belonged to a well-known club. He turned and, still standing there, faced their neighbour's flat; the nameplate on the door simply said 'Ghosh'. The man, whom Jayojit had seen no more than a couple of times, apparently ran some kind of small business in timber, and was often away in the hilly, presently strife-torn area of Assam (and yet how lovely and green and misty Assam had been when he'd gone visiting relatives with parents once as a boy); and his thin grey-haired wife, Jayojit's mother had said, was called Pramila. Relations with the Chatterjees were cordial,

41

if minimal. In all kinds of ways, these people were a million miles away from Jayojit's parents and their world; their ambitions were different, their friends and referents were different, even the Bengali they spoke was different; they might have belonged to different countries. The lack of contact was also perhaps partly Jayojit's family's fault. For, since the divorce, the Admiral and his wife had withdrawn into themselves and gone into a sort of mourning; their flat had become a shell, and the neighbours' flat, in their imagination, had moved further away. And yet, during that great leveller, the Durga Puja, Jayojit's mother apparently met Mr and Mrs Ghosh downstairs at the festivities, became part of a crowd where all disparity and private, secluding grief were temporarily suspended, and were even delighted to 'bump into' each other and exchange meaningless small talk during the three-day-long ceremonies. Each year it provided a brief but vivid illusion of life beginning again, to which everyone succumbed. What Jayojit could see now, as he stood here, was the back door to the Ghoshes' kitchen, a door with criss-cross netting through which part of a crate and a bench were visible. It was true that they weren't socially compatible, that before the Admiral's retirement their chances of meeting would have been remote, the Admiral with his command belonging to a different world altogether; but this country had a way of, in the end, concealing disparity and banishing the past.

'Careful, don't hit the door,' said Jayojit as Bonny began to play on that side of the corridor. His son looked up at him and continued to improvise his little game.

Jayojit could feel now, after two and a half weeks, that he was putting on weight. A suspicion found its way to his head which he'd never harboured before: had his father become so bulky because his mother had overfed him during his working life? He'd always assumed that his father, at some point in his life, had inadvertently eaten too much; but now he wondered if his mother had deliberately played a part. As for Bonny, he, with Jayojit's approval, had moved, by the end of the first week, to the breakfasts he was used to having; cereal (a box of Champion Oats had been procured, when they'd been convinced these were no longer available, by the Admiral, with both perseverance and faith, from New Market), a glass of milk, fruit juice—the consoling and rare sweet lime, one of which yielded only a quarter glass of juice and for whose taste Bonny had no appreciation at all; though his grandmother kept trying to tempt him towards the luchis, cajoling and pleading with him.

'Don't force him, ma,' said Jayojit with an indulgent sternness. 'Don't spoil him—he's not used to oily meals of this kind in the mornings.'

She listened to him, abashed, as if *he* were her mother. In America he'd imbibed clear ideas, while having no idea that he had, of what to eat and what not to. Jayojit also wanted to spare her from preparing these breakfasts—she seemed to have a dogged capacity, even at this age, for working in the heat—but feeding her own son, really, seemed to give her pleasure at a time when hardly anything mattered to her. She would come out from the kitchen, her sari tightly wound around her, her face flushed. Although she appeared so submissive, there was a streak of obstinacy in her—both Jayojit and his father knew this. She would never make clear what conclusions she had reached emotionally, and, in everything, would cannily refer to the Admiral, either repeating what he said, or saying, 'Ask him.'

By eight-thirty, when they had breakfast, the dining and sitting rooms would be hot; it was a miracle they could sit and eat here every day, registering no discomfort except a few loud exclamations about the heat. Dawn would end at half-past five, and the day had had ample time to become hot by eight-thirty.

Two weeks on, Jayojit explained to his mother, 'From tomorrow, I'm going to have toast and tea—no more!' For he could feel the shape of his body changing; and he was afraid of triglycerides showing up in his bloodstream, as they had in some of his friends.

'O ma—what's this!' she said in surprise. 'But you don't even eat much for lunch! You must at least have one proper meal a day.'

'Ma, I've been eating better than I have for months—' and he meant it.

For two weeks he'd done little but read newspapers, and desired, in secret, to finish a book, until he sat before his laptop in the afternoon, with the chiks in the balcony more than three-quarters of the way down to keep out the heat. The chiks moved lightly, as if someone had just pushed them.

The screen lighted up; he browsed slowly through old files, his mind elsewhere. Every time he'd tried to return to, during the last two months, the project he was supposed to be working on, he found himself trying to escape it like a boy in a classroom drawn to looking out of a window during a lesson.

Before him, on the wall, there was a batik print of Ganesh that served the dual, not incompatible, purpose of being a decoration and bringing good fortune to the house. Beneath it, there was a table covered with a Rajasthani cloth with mirrorwork upon it. Each circle of glass reflected some bit of the room, no longer recognizable, independent of whatever it was it represented. These things had been bought on an impulse long ago—but the print was fairly recent—and had not so much to do with serious thought or judgement as trespassing into emporia and feeling heartless about leaving empty-handed. Then there was a Kashmiri shikara, slightly removed from its place, which is how Maya sometimes left things after she'd dusted them.

On the table there were photographs: one of Jayojit at the age of nineteen, become thin and tall (he had been pudgy as a boy), wearing thick black-framed spectacles, which were fashionable in those days; he was then at the Hindu College. Another of Jayojit and his brother Ranajit when they were thirteen and ten respectively, taken on a holiday in Madhya Pradesh, both the boys, in their long pants and keds, looking like colonizers on that ancient terrain; a wedding photo, bright with colour, of Ranajit and his wife. There were other smaller photographs, of cousins and relatives, and a series of pictures, in a large frame, of Bonny at different stages of his life; as a baby, as a child of two, when his hair, mysteriously, had been curlier than it was now, a boy of four in trousers with braces. The wedding pictures had disappeared, or become oddly improper. The pictures of Bonny were sans parents, as if he'd been conceived in a future when parents were not only no longer necessary, but were no more possible.

The only other picture of a couple among those photographs was one of Jayojit's parents. It had been taken on their twenty-fifth marriage anniversary. The Admiral was noticeably less heavy in the photograph than now, his hair and beard a little less long. She was smiling faintly, almost shyly. Then there was a picture of the Admiral in uniform, taken some time in the eighties, a few years before Jayojit got married. There were also, separately, pictures of the Admiral's parents; one of his mother and another of his father. Faded and obscure, and to all purposes forgotten, they still didn't seem insignificant; they lived not in some afterlife, but some moment in history as difficult to imagine now as this moment would have been to imagine then. In its own and different way, that time must have been as shadowy and uncertain as any now, struggling, as well, to arrive at its brief being and truth; everything about that world must have been disequilibrious and dark to Jayojit's grandfather. Jayojit knew that his grandfather had once run away from home to seek spiritual truth, and later, for some reason, returned to his parents. Then, not content to inherit land and his father's estates, he'd gone to Dhaka and then to Calcutta and become a successful journalist. Thus, Jayojit's father had been born in Calcutta, somewhere in the north, where it was impossible to go now because of the traffic. Jayojit himself had never seen his father's mother; his father's father had died when he was three.

His mother's parents he could remember well. For years they used to live in a small mining town in Bihar. Sometimes he'd go to them with both his parents, sometimes with his mother. He'd notice, then, how fragile and unthinking his mother's relationship seemed to be with his grandparents, how forgetful she became when she was with them, and then longed to go back after a month had passed, as if she had grown tired because she'd never completely be a girl again.

Once, when typing, he thought there was someone else in the room; looking up, he realized it was one of his mother's saris, washed but not pressed, left in a bundle on the sofa; it had become a form on the edge of his vision. He looked up from the screen and gazed at the chik that was three-quarters of the way down to keep out the heat. Again and again, but with no obvious regularity in the intervals, the chik stirred, creaked, with the sigh of a south-easterly breeze; and beyond, the guttural murmurs of idle drivers, the punctilious beating of metal, hovered with an air of expectancy.

That afternoon, he went out for a walk again; restless, with nothing to do, wondering how long the two months (of which thirteen days had gone already) would last. As he was setting out, he saw a group of schoolchildren returning in blue and white uniforms. They loitered in the hall before walking towards the lift; they seemed to be without a sense of urgency.

He walked past them, and he might have been invisible in his off-white trousers and check shirt. As he came into the sun, he narrowed his eyes instinctively.

He recalled that, as a child, he'd never known the meaning of this daily homecoming from school; instead, he'd wait till summer, say goodbye to his friends in Ooty (Aniruddha Sen, his constant companion in the Ninth Standard, came to mind undiminished with his long nose; apparently he was now a financial consultant in Birmingham), or postpone saying goodbye indefinitely, as the case might be (because promotions and the perpetual upward journey through new classes hurt almost physically when he was a boy, like a pang of birth), and then take a train to wherever his father happened to be posted. And then his mother would dote on him, almost consolingly, for two months, making not luchis as she did now single-handedly, but the cook preparing exotic rubbish: sweetcorn on toast; or versions of the roadside junk-food that was otherwise taboo to him.

This had been the subject of jocular ribbing in the early days with Amala.

'There's a limit to carefulness, baba,' she'd said, rolling her eyes, for she herself had grown up in a family that allowed her to try out everything once; indeed, apparently she and her mother ventured out together in search of golgappas, getting out of their Ambassador near the vendors at Deshapriya Park.

He came to the main road now, confronted a tram, and turned right. This city irritated him; it was like an obstacle; yet he'd decided that it would give him the space for recoupment that he thought was necessary now. Nothing had changed from a year ago; only the pavement here seemed more dusty than he'd remembered and was like a path that ran parallel to the road. He walked on, until he saw three familiar shops in the distance, on the left, on the other side; a provisions store, a fast-food outlet, and a drugstore. He felt not so much a sense of déjà vu as one of ironic, qualified continuity. Then, further off, he saw a hoarding above a busy and troubled junction, where a stream of cars was divided into two or more directions, the conjunctive but disparate existences of Ballygunge Circular and Hazra roads, and saw that it had an advertisement, the same as last time, aimed at which set of eyes and personalities he didn't know, for the ATM. The Hong Kong Bank copywriters had interpreted the ATM as Any

Time Money, and it was the same advertisement except that it was a fresh slogan. It hovered in mid-air above a razed and derelict island.

He remembered his father saying to him during a telephone conversation, sounding as if the whole truth hadn't sunk in: 'Joy, are you sure I shouldn't call her parents? Mr Chakraborty could talk some sense into her …'

'Baba, there's nothing to salvage,' he'd said, patiently waiting for the line to clear. 'It's finished.' He had to say this to remind himself it was so. 'What worries me now,' he'd continued calmly, 'is that she has Bonny with her.' To reassure his father at the other end, he'd said, 'Listen, I'll call you tomorrow to tell you what I'm doing about that.'

That evening he'd said to her when she'd phoned him, 'You know, I could call the police.' Without realizing it, he'd stopped calling her by her name, and hardly ever did so later. She, however, had begun to use his name as if it were a weapon with which she could now distance herself from him: 'Why, what'll you tell them, Joy?' Her voice was mock-serious.

He felt somewhat conspicuous as he turned back; he didn't know why. Perhaps because people don't wander about and not go anywhere; perhaps this was what made him feel strange and doubtful and that he stood out. Everyone else, whatever they looked like, had somewhere to go to, or seemed to; and if they were doing nothing or postponing doing something, as some of these people squatting by the pavement, who seemed to be in part-time employment, were doing, it was for a reason. But the small journey—in the heat, constantly assailed by traffic on the Ballygunge main road—and then the small arc back had somewhat settled his thoughts. No, it was still new to him, that's what it was; as if he'd just stepped off the plane and this was his first day out, and everything—or this web that constituted, at the moment, 'everything'—seemed louder and more real to him than normal.

Ballygunge is, he conceded with the uncertainty of one who has been acquainted with better places, in its way, beautiful. His parents knew people here once; and he concluded, without evidence to support him, that some of those people must be here, in these flats and houses. Why did they never meet: or did they, while he simply knew nothing about it? On the other hand, it might be that what they'd lived in—those compact decorated spaces—were company flats, in which case they might have moved to other parts of the city; another part of the country, even. A peasant in a dhoti and a turban was sitting on the pavement next to a makeshift cigarette stall and lighting a bidi with one of those ropes that burned stubbornly at the end.

As he turned into the lane he had to step aside adroitly for a car coming in; it blew its horn behind him.

A new Ambassador, a recent model that could have sprung, unchanged, from the older one, newly painted, its cream colour not yet dirty except for two indistinguishable scratches on the side; at the back, a girl whose age hovered anywhere between seventeen and twenty-one—in which case it was insulting to think of her as a girl, for no doubt she saw herself as a woman—managing her long, straight hair with an expert flick of her head.

Jayojit stared at the back of her head as it grew smaller. The car passed a bhelpuri vendor and Jayojit wondered if it would stop to make a purchase. No, it did not. Blowing its horn again, it turned right at the end of the lane.

But it's a nice area, he decided generously; deceptively quiet. Nothing seemed to happen here in these mansions which belonged to people who'd once made a tidy sum of money. Money creates money; you could sense that as you went past the houses and their tall, imposing gates. The owners of these mansions had guaranteed their own self-perpetuating well-being, it seemed, for generations to come. Independence, the subsequent changes of history, did not seem to matter.

This one, for instance, impressive, especially in light of the fact that such a large house must be tremendously expensive to maintain; the bold letters JHUNJHUNWALA painted by the gate, a gecko, at a curious angle, meditating on the letters. Who was Jhunjhunwala?—Jayojit felt he should have known the name if only to ridicule it, to retrieve, from an uncertain memory, a nasty item of gossip, but it did not matter. There must be about ten or fifteen rooms in there—the curtains were drawn—with air-conditioners protruding at the back.

He came to the end of the lane, where the Ambassador had turned not long ago, where he saw a house that had once been equally impressive if not more. The name on the gate, he noticed, was that of an East Bengali landowner; but East Bengal had long ago been transformed into fantasy; the driveway was covered with leaves that no one had bothered to clear away; space and an impartially surviving light co-existed in equilibrium before the awning. No one had even bothered to sell the house.

The bhelpuri seller fussing and making his preparations; but all his movements were actually well judged and accurate. Before him his adult life's work, and the day's; the tamarind water, the crackers that he would crush, scattering the flakes on his small concoction. A portable investment; he didn't need to be confined to any one place. But he had a clientele in this locality; he was waiting for it to make an appearance.

Jayojit walked back some of the way he'd come, as if retracing his route, and passed the man; the man noticed him with his apparently unintrusive abstracted eyes; he judged, him, not unfriendlily, as a potential, a probable, customer; a loiterer who might also be integrated with his market. He made the first move, possibly making his first enquiry of the afternoon. His eyes were brown-grey, as if they held a little of the twilight of another town in them.

'Bhelpuri, babu? Jhaalmudi?' Tapping the market with all the finesse of a researcher and the seductiveness of an old retainer; trying to increase his clientele, though it doesn't matter to him one way or the other.

'Kato?' The Bengali word for 'How much' seemed out of place, too tentative and non-committal.

'Bhelpuri, babu?'

'Hay bhelpuri.'

'Dui taka'—two rupees.

An absurd price, almost as close to nothing as words themselves; but the confection must cost even less to make. Jayojit nodded and walked on, as if he'd been doing a survey; the man smiled slightly, not even a smile of puzzlement, but of the acceptance of one whose curiosity was already waning.

There were birds in the trees overhead, all shouting together. He remembered how he and Amala had, when visiting India (their visits home were regular and annual for the first three years), gone to Nainital in the second year of their marriage, to the wildlife sanctuary, hoping to be amazed by the glimpse of some rare beast—all beasts were rare to them—or the sight of a peacock dancing. What had struck Jayojit then more than anything else was the crescendo caused by the birds' chattering and crying at dusk. At night, in the hotel, they'd been bitten by mosquitoes, and while examining Amala's mosquito bites from the feet upwards—there was a bite on the thigh, in spite of the fact that she was wearing a salwaar kameez; 'How the hell did it get *there?*' she'd asked—there was a preamble that led to love-making, in which they'd almost forgotten about the mosquitoes. That was in 1986. Two years after Bonny's birth in March 1987 (he would have been conceived a few months after they'd gone back from India to Claremont) their love-making dried up, almost without their noticing it. At first they joked about it, she laughing: 'Think we should get into partner-swapping?'; he, when

Amala occasionally took the initiative: 'What? You want to interrupt *Dallas*?' Sometimes, when Bonny'd just learnt how to speak, they'd kiss each other, even in front of the boy. Then unfamiliarity set in, though no one else would notice it, and they got used to even that. The child, instead of bringing them together, actually enabled them to separate into their own spheres of desire and loneliness. All along, whenever they quarrelled, they quarrelled with great precision in the English they'd grown up with; Bonny, smaller then, would listen to their analyses of each other with wandering attention, as if he were overhearing a foreign language.

What he judged most harshly was that Amala should get involved with her gynaecologist, himself a married man. He found Amala's transformation impossible to understand or interpret; equally strange her claim, 'He was kind to me.' He'd been with Amala himself to this doctor before Bonny's birth; a not unpleasant-looking man in his forties who was balding slightly, and surely not charismatic; a whiff of bad breath reached Jayojit from his conversation once; difficult, almost impossible, to imagine how any woman in her right mind could prefer him to Jayojit; and later, Jayojit had said as much to the Admiral. Still later, thinking of this, the Admiral had quietly quoted a proverb to Jayojit in Sanskrit, translating himself: 'Of woman's character and man's fate even God is ignorant; what knowledge then can mortals have of these things?'

When Jayojit had gone back to the end of the lane, marching behind the shadows of the trees towards the main road, and turned back, he saw two boys emerge from the gates of the building and advance towards the bhelpuri seller: wearing t-shirts and shorts and keds, casually decisive. There was the slightest premonition of dusk.

Abrupt high-pitched voices, asking the man to serve up his stuff; the man only too eager to please, but inwardly composed, seeming to experience something like satisfaction; then wiping his hands slowly on an old and rather dirty piece of cloth.

'Jaldi, jaldi.' Impatience.

He himself felt tempted, but he'd promised himself not to get diarrhoea or gastro-enteritis if he could help it; or wind.

The two boys were busy.

The dhobi—returning washed and ironed clothes to Jayojit's mother. He sat near the front door and untied his bundle. Jayojit, for some reason, had a memory of him; no, it couldn't be last time he'd seen him—he must have seen him downstairs. He lifted the items of clothing, with a detached saintly air, but with an unobtrusive cunning as well, one by one and handed them to Mrs Chatterjee, who inspected each with suspicion. It reminded Jayojit of the way he'd seen her, in the past, examining 'bargains' with a tired but amenable gaze in various shops. Clean sheets, folded on top of each other, saris, pressed and starched, crisp with the heat; there were few things to rival washed clothes in their undisappointing recurrence.

'It's the humidity I hate,' said Jayojit, fanning himself, without warning, with a piece of paper. 'I wonder, especially, if it's good for you, baba.'

The Admiral said nothing at this feeling of concern, unsought for; he watched with interest as his wife went inside their room, delayed reappearing, and came out with small change to pay the dhobi.

'Baba,' said Jayojit suddenly, with his eyes on the newspaper, 'couldn't one have got a flat on the other side?' He pointed to the right. 'I've heard they're slightly larger there—and cooler as well.' In fact he'd heard this piece of information from his mother. It now intrigued him.

The Admiral looked puzzled for a moment. 'Yes, those flats *are* south facing,' he said, abstracted, as if he could see a flat before his eyes. He tried to remember, as one remembers a fact that has lost its original importance and place, but nevertheless cannot be forgotten, and said, 'There was a … a—what do they call it—a lottery. We applied late.'

But Jayojit was not listening; he was momentarily absorbed in a report. He was nodding, but probably at something the reporter had said.

The Admiral had been posted at Cochin at the time he had booked the flat; the building had still not come up at the time. A 'friend' of his called Dutta had, for some reason he could never fathom, phoned him and given him, at the time—1972—the information about the building. 'Excellent flats. The building's a government project, so it's cheap. I'd advise you to act immediately, because there's a great rush of middle-class buyers. Do you understand?' Strange, the people who do you a good turn; some of them don't even matter to you; they come and go, like bit-players. Where was Dutta now? The Admiral didn't really care; he had little time, anyway, to turn his gaze upon minor aspects of the past. But thank God for that phone call! That was a different country then, in the seventies, and his posting in Cochin, when one looked back on it, a paid holiday with grand trappings; there was glory too for the armed forces, because of the war over Bangladesh, though the navy didn't really have to take part; it had just sat and watched with dignity. No one knew then how unaffordable property would be, especially now; how fortunate one was to have a home. And there was no 'black' money involved because it was a government scheme; but it was a stroke of good luck that the Admiral had been successful in his application without bribes or pulling strings. But, in those years, he hadn't seen it as good luck, he'd almost expected, in a naive, trusting way, nothing else.

From the proposal to the final construction of the building, when the rooms became habitable, it had taken five years. Whenever the Admiral was in Calcutta in that period (to attend a function or visit some relative; to be put up at Fort William or at some relative's place), he would come to this lane to take a look at the building as it came up, first the skeleton of the construction, then the gaps where the rooms were. He found the process oddly interesting and involving; it wasn't always one had the opportunity to watch a vision, however ordinary, take shape. The lane, with the post office nearby, and the stately old mansions that were still there now, was subtly different; it was as if the lane were, in its way, passing from one phase of its history to another, in a way that was somehow connected to the completion of the building and his being there, a reticent but attentive witness.

What would happen in the future? Jayojit couldn't see himself returning once his parents weren't there, or ever settling down here himself—he'd gone too far into the continent of his domicile and been absorbed by it; and imagine the foolhardiness of returning to India! But his parents ending up here must be considered both fortunate, he thought, and one of the anomalies of life.

Jayojit took off his glasses and wiped the lenses that had misted over with perspiration. His face bore a remarkable similarity to his father's, the same lines around the mouth, the nose curving gently, the same fair complexion, both faces marked by education, a privileged background, and, it was clear, some sort of achievement. The father's was a brahmin's face, rather old-fashioned in a way; in another setting, another time, it would have had a worldly but ceremonial aura; it had an inherited severity. The grey hairs on his beard had a frosty stillness. In both faces, especially on the father's, there was a trace of dissatisfaction and naivety, suggesting that neither man could make friends easily.

The Admiral asked:

'Did you read the news today?'

The dhobi had gone. Jayojit's mother had some of the folded clothes in her arms; like a familiar spirit, she was carrying them inside. In the trees outside, there was the sound of the constantly busy birds.

'Something about a British delegation,' said Jayojit. 'Coming to survey their old territory.' He chuckled. 'News' was still strange to him, like the repetitive cry of one of the shalik birds outside, an echo. When he was in Claremont, he kept track of everything that happened here, and his thoughts about this country had a completeness they no longer had once he was back.

'I don't see the point, really. What do they intend to do: inspect the roads? You know they won't really welcome them with open arms. The Chief Minister isn't the problem. The trade unions and the party cadres are the problem! Do you think they'll allow it? Not to speak of the hooligans in the Congress.' The Admiral had a sneaking, unconfessed admiration for the Chief Minister because he'd done his Bar-at-Law in England; he was a 'gentleman'. Then, in Bengali, he said: 'Meanwhile, look what's happening to this city. You can't walk on the pavement, can't post a letter.' In English again, seriously, 'I wouldn't advise *you* to come back to it.'

Jayojit's mother returned to broodingly retrieve the last load of laundered articles; 'She's become a household machine,' thought Jayojit, a little unfairly, as her shadow passed by him, 'maybe she's happy this way.' He knew how often she used to go shopping at the JK Market with her friend Manju in Delhi.

'I'm afraid there isn't much chance of that in the near future,' said Jayojit to his father, and laughed, as if he had just remembered something.

The Admiral's thoughts had moved on; he was staring into the distance. 'You remember Bijon,' he said suddenly.

Jayojit started out of his own thoughts. Bijon used to work in an engineering firm in Delhi; his aquaintance with the Admiral was through some tenuous but palpable route; Jayojit's mother's late brother-in-law's niece had a husband whose sister had married Bijon, who himself had no children; or some such laborious relationship. Somehow Bijon and the Admiral had become occasional drinking partners at the Services Club (the

Admiral had now, that is, for the last six years, perforce, given up drinking).

'Why?' As if some private, guarded realm had somehow been violated by the question. Then: 'No, of course I remember him.'

Bijon was supposed to have retired about two years ago and moved to Calcutta. He was not what one would call close to the Admiral; but over drinks they'd exchanged confidences that were self-revelatory in nature. You needed someone to exchange confidences with; even the Admiral.

'He's gone to Dubai,' said the Admiral.

'Really?'

That hadn't been part of the plan; but things seldom were. It was as if the Admiral had somehow been betrayed. He spoke of him as if he were a desert mirage, something quite ordinary that had turned out to be odd only by being insubstantial, arising and then fading in a vaguely recognizable, uncategorizable foreign landscape.

Early in the morning, when the Admiral and his wife woke up, they didn't at first say a word to each other; it was as if they didn't feel the need to. Above, the fan turned at full speed, giving the Admiral, for once, mild goose-flesh as he emerged from the night's sheets. They had it planned between them; that Admiral Chatterjee would go in for his bath first, and then be the one to open the doors to the verandah in the sitting room. Two or three loud coughs administered his entry into the sitting room, refamiliarized him with its tidiness, its claim to be accessory to his present life; these coughs were physical but ritual in nature; in the other bedroom, neither Jayojit nor Bonny heard him over the internal hum of the air-conditioner. When they weren't there, the coughs were directed at a nervous sense of absence, at the faraway. The Admiral then went in for a bath of cold water, water gathered in a bucket with which he then drenched himself from head to bottom, which he believed would keep him cool and sane for the rest of the morning; even his sacred thread, which he neglected to remove, became soggy. He didn't like being disturbed in the midst of his quick ablutions, but this was more an idea than a reasonable suspicion, because there was no possibility that he would be. In the bedroom, Mrs Chatterjee, very softly, as she often did these days, or ever since she had grown used to this negligible but returning loneliness, turned on the transistor radio to listen to devotionals. Something about these bhajans was apposite to her semi-wakefulness of the first half-hour of getting out of bed.

Then they went to walk in the lane with the air of those who'd grown, lately, accustomed to a routine, but still weren't entirely reconciled to what the day might bring. They looked bourgoise and ascetic; as if walking in the silence were a polite activity not unrelated to some unrealizable desire for completeness. There were no cars to disturb them now; and if a car did enter the lane from the main road, the Admiral stood aside gravely to let it pass, while Mrs Chatterjee, unmindful, last morning's vermilion faded in her hair's parting, went a little way ahead; though no one saw them, the Admiral behaved with an impatient propriety, uncommunicable to her, in relation to his wife, as if someone who mattered to him were watching them. They walked to one end of the lane, the birds shrieking above them; nothing had begun; only a couple of cleaners were in view, who, with buckets, had just begun washing the parked cars and wiping their windows.

It was impossible to tell from what it was like now just how hot it would become in two hours; this was one of the small deceptions of this time of the year. Even the trees and leaves and the sudden burst of gulmohurs kept them from this fact as they walked underneath them.

Seven years ago, with the mild stroke, there had been a fleeting fear of paralysis; the Admiral's right arm, the old saluting arm, had been mildly affected. Then, with physiotherapy and a gradual rationalizing of that fear, that had passed. Ridiculous—to have survived the Indo-Chinese conflict and the Pakistan wars, not only survived them, but to have contemplated them from some distance; and then to be cut down, not in battle, but by the excesses of one's past—drinking, hypertension! Now, these new and old buildings, the new ones looking quite unfamiliar at this time of the day, rose around them. The Admiral remembered Mrs Gupta's husband who used to live on the seventh storey of their building, flat 7C, who'd had a stroke and one side of his face paralysed; and lived like that for six years. No longer here; he had died last February.

The vibrating sound of trams was not far away; he'd been advised to take walks by two different doctors, one in the army hospital and another one, Dr Sen, who lived in this building. 'You can walk your way into health, sir,' the army doctor had said. And he felt like a young long-distance runner, cut off from both onlookers and competitors, engaged in a personal struggle; he felt this need to see Jayojit through; Jayojit was too hot-headed for his own good, that had become apparent.

The thought of his other son, the younger one, Ranajit, married (happily, he hoped!) for four years and living in the arborous suburb, Vasant Vihar, in Delhi, disturbed him only remotely, as would a story he was reading with interest, but mainly to get to the end. No sign of children as yet; his daughter-in-law, Anita, was twenty-seven years old; couples waited and waited these days for the opportune moment to arrive as if it were some kind of secret, as if they were gamblers hedging their bets endlessly. Of course Ranajit didn't tell him everything, and he wrote infrequently; he and Anita might be planning something— you 'planned' everything these days, the husband and wife not so much conspirators but like bureaucrats in a command economy; unlike thirty or forty years ago; Ranajit and Jayojit hadn't been planned or expected, they'd just 'happened'—and neither the Admiral nor his wife would know until later.

He'd like Jayojit to marry again. Joy was thirty-seven; he wasn't young any more. If he married now, the Admiral believed, it would be like attending to a wound when it was still fresh.

It was probably tendentious to think of it in that way, but if it hadn't been for Bonny the match they'd organized last year might have worked. It wasn't Bonny's *fault* of course; it was just the way these things were. The Admiral was not orthodoxly religious— though he believed in the laws according to which providential happiness was given or withheld, and would sometimes return from a temple with a tilak beneath the mane of hair that had not long ago been hidden by a naval officer's cap—and yet he'd hoped for an alliance with both the devotee's humility and his serene expectation of disappointment; when the disappointment came, it took him by surprise. But that girl, Arundhati, had insisted that she found Bonny perfectly charming. 'What d'you want to be when you grow up, Bonny?' she'd asked him, sitting forward on a sofa as he stood before her, plates of onion savouries on the table, a pale glass of lemon sharbat in her hand; and when he answered, at last, 'I don't know,' they'd laughed as if it were the most knowing, canny answer to the question.

'If you don't mind my asking, how long did it last?' Jayojit had asked during one of their conversations, although he already had a fair idea from the person who'd introduced them. The aura of that marriage had preceded her, the story with vague correspondences to his own; all this related by a nondescript go-between, a gentleman wearing bifocals who worked at the middle level of a tea company. She lived on the ground floor of a house with a terrace, somewhere near a park on a by-lane not far from Southern Avenue; here, on the verandah, facing the dark horizon of the park, they were left to themselves (Bonny would be at home with his grandparents), not far from the lit windows of a neighbouring house. She had, in an unostentatious way, attended to herself before his visit, put on lipstick, an outline of kohl, and something on her face that made it pale against the dark.

There had been a pause; and then, dismissing the memory the question might have brought to her, she'd said:

'One year.' She was pouring him tea.

'That's a bloody short time, if you don't mind my saying,' said forcefully to convey his indignation not at her but her former husband.

Then she'd told him how (still conveying to him something of her disbelief), after going to London with her husband, who was studying medicine there, she'd be left alone in the house without any money. They were in a house on Golders Green; he commuted each morning to King's College Hospital. She used to sit watching television, or go for long walks. 'Actually,' smiling, 'I went to Oxford Street only thrice. I didn't see the Tower of London or Westminster Abbey. I wanted to go to the Tower to see all the jewels the Brits took from us and put on their crowns and—what do they call them—sceptres.'

The clattering of cutlery could be heard inside. After a polite search for a cue, he'd asked her, returning her, without warning, to the present:

'What's the park like?' He regarded it in the partial illumination; it seemed both sinister and peaceful. She seemed slightly flustered, as if he'd crossed a boundary and said something personal.

'Oh, the park ...' She didn't know how to put it to him without sounding melodramatic. 'It isn't safe any more. I haven't been to it for years ... When I was a child, it was quite nice, though ...'

Later, they'd gone in and joined her parents inside; the mother dressed in a tangail sari, the father bespectacled, sipping tea nervously, their shadow on the wall, excited by innocent speculation, partaking of the new romance as if they were at the cinema. They had tea at their own table guiltily. A car passed by outside, lighting the lane and the trees with its headlights.

She was a junior advertising executive; her parents nowhere near as well-to-do as Amala's. Yet when he asked her what the job was like, she'd say no more than, 'It's quite nice,' as if her vocabulary had deserted her with the effort of readjusting to this city (she'd lived here, now, for a little more than two years). Or it was probably that she was too respectful of his accomplishments, his achievements. That was during their third meeting in two weeks. He'd begun to like talking to her; the similar traumas they'd suffered had made them uninquisitive about each other, and comfortable about their small silences.

She might be in the same job (Jayojit was wondering the other day, daydreaming as he seldom did); or moved to another company (as if there were so many other advertising companies to move to in this city in which business had ebbed into a low tide!); or—the last possibility was the likeliest—she might have got married, remarried, with fewer bonds to bind her to her past life than he still had, crossed a bridge really, in which case she need not necessarily be in this city, she might be in another.

They had met once again, soon after, at a wedding. 'Really? And how are you related ...' She in a Bomkai sari (though he was no good at spotting sub-species of women's garments; his mother had identified it later), exuding a kind of gratitude at his being there.

He, perspiring, had explained his slender acquaintance, through his parents, with the bridegroom. They might have been making their way through a dark wilderness, so little time did they have alone with each other.

Light reflected off the cars; their hoods were getting hot. On the main road, buses that were now beginning to get half-full were rushing onward with great urgency. The people in them were already hot, already anxious. The cleaners, by now, had finished their work and a few other latecomers had begun.

They decided to go up; the Admiral glanced at his watch; it, this Swiss watch with its off-white dial he'd had for years, as remote and familiar as a morning star, said it was a quarter to seven. They'd walked for too long; both of them were certain that Jayojit must be awake. Who would give him tea? thought his father; annoyed with his wife for not having uttered this question. The istriwalla watched them without actually seeing them, as if the morning had made them invisible; and the watchman fumbled and seemed to be waiting for a change to come and take his place. What a young boy he was ... probably nineteen.

When evening came, loud conversations came from other flats, of which even whispers were audible. Sometimes the voices became agitated, or were interrupted by music, or there was a roar at times that turned out to be applause; everything was exaggerated, and not quite commensurate with whatever it was that the sounds were representing.

Behind this, ancient but entirely of the present, was the sound of crickets.

Jayojit had been lying on the sofa, reading, fatigued by the weather, until, hearing a noise in the lane, he got up to see what it was and locate it. But it wasn't possible to see much of the lane from the verandah; only a section of it was visible through the trees.

'Baba, can I look?' Bonny was standing next to him; he came to no higher than his father's waist. He stood on tiptoe and arched his back.

'There's nothing to see,' said Jayojit. Cars were being parked—it was obvious from the continual and sudden sound of the horns—and the side of a Maruti, shining dully, could just be seen. In the small bit of the lane which they could see, women in silk saris, flickering in the bad light of the lane, passed by. From behind, the Admiral peered out, unappeasable but stoic, and went back in again.

They could hear the shehnai. It was a tape, for soon the same raags began to be played again.

'This is not the best time of the year to get married, surely,' declared Jayojit, waving a housefly away with excessive displeasure, as he turned from the verandah; Bonny was still craning his neck outward, his chin above the bannister, hoping to somehow make his face fit into part of the jigsaw puzzle of the grille.

'It's the Marwari house next to the building,' said Jayojit's mother, her face turned away from him. 'That big one.'

Jayojit did not know the one she meant. He'd explored from the outside the large houses like memorials in the lane, but hadn't seen the one next to the building, or perhaps his memory had refused to give individuality to the neighbouring houses.

'I should have known.' He made a face, as if disparaging the wastefulness of the community mentioned, but from the safety and distance of irony, without quite the crude derision he'd overheard in conversations.

They ate at eight-thirty; they would seldom eat later because of the Admiral's health. Behind the sound of the cutlery—the Admiral habitually made a lot of noise, like one busily dispatching a meal in a railway canteen—the shehnai could be heard, high-pitched, almost intrusive; and then a watchman's voice on a loudspeaker announcing the numbers of cars, speaking an urgent Hindustani version of English letters and numbers, became audible.

'But who lives in that house?' asked Jayojit, midway through a spoonful of rice.

'I don't know their name,' said his mother.

'No, no, not that one,' gesturing to the noise. 'I meant the other big one opposite. The Jhunjhunwala house.'

The Admiral looked up; he had been chewing on a small piece of vegetable. 'His father started out as a supplier to the automobile industry'—he held up one hand as Jayojit snorted, 'What automobile industry!'—'and now they're in all kinds of things including cement.'

'A-ha!' as if this had confirmed the essential murkiness behind the existence of that mansion.

'Can I have some daal, tamma?' Bonny, his gaze nervous and transparent, surprised at his own voice, looked askance at his grandmother, who leaned forward to serve him.

'Wonder of wonders,' said Jayojit, reaching ostentatiously and serving himself some vegetables. Behind his exaggerated movements was also a returning pain, not so much a backache or an ache in the joints as a discomfort that he was repeatedly trying to exorcise. 'I didn't know you had an appetite.'

'He has investments abroad,' said the Admiral, continuing undeterred about Jhunjhunwala.

Bonny was only eating daal; this mild gruel, with one green chilli afloat in it, had become the most desired, sometimes the only, component of his everyday diet. It seemed to demand less of him and leave him alone; and, instinctively realizing this, both his father and grandmother pretended not to care about the unvarying nature of his food. Fish-bones he had trouble with; he only accepted bhetki, and that didn't always come from the market.

He finished before the rest were done, and got up and went to the far side of the sitting room and, dabbling with the remote control, turned to MTV; unconcerned that the volume was low, he sat on the rug before it. The sound of the shehnai mixed with this other sound; a succession of images, quicker than a train of association, hurried through the screen. For the Admiral and Mrs Chatterjee, the television was always on in the evening until a year ago; it didn't matter if they were watching it or not; the colours of one of the five channels, a rainbow of the chatter and information of the new India, kept changing in one corner of the room. Then, last year, during the second, prolonged custody battle, they'd neglected a couple of episodes of a soap, forgot, as if they'd inadvertently swallowed a pill that erased recent memory, whether Hersh was sleeping with Jordan (you couldn't tell, from the names, which sex who belonged to) or Richard had finally deserted Anastasia; they'd found they could no longer immerse themselves, or even find a centre, however temporary, in a proxy existence. One day, three months ago, when Mrs Chatterjee was sitting absently before the TV with the remote control in her hand (she could never fathom how best to use it; she couldn't cope with the choice it presented to her, and suffered when it was in her control), she saw a face and heard a voice that was dimly familiar. The blonde, sturdy jawed woman was someone she'd met before: it was Anastasia. She was filled with longing for a bygone simplicity.

The next morning Jayojit woke up at eight, still sleepy. 'Did they keep you awake?' he asked, scratching his stubble. 'I fell asleep,' confessed the Admiral.

The rest of the day was hot and surprisingly silent. Late last night the lane had echoed, even when the shehnai had died away, with the loudspeaker, imperative and muffled, announcing numbers. Jayojit had caught himself listening to them again in the bathroom as his head jangled to the sound of his own toothbrush. This morning he'd discovered the bathroom light on, its lustre wasted in daylight. He thought ephemerally of the Marwari bridegroom and his new wife, imagined what they might look like, of the wife's comeliness, and her shyness inevitably wearing away the way the light in the bathroom had merged into the daylight's ordinariness, and that the two might even be preparing to get on to a plane. He read the papers twice, bored the first time, with the writing and with life in India, and in a more interested way the second time round; then he read an article about how well Indians were doing 'abroad'; naturally, by 'abroad' the reporter meant not so much Kuwait or Bangladesh but principally America. He not so much disagreed with it as felt the report belonged to another era, another planet. How naive and innocent and ultimately patronizing and misleading everything in it was! After he'd finished, he suddenly missed the vigilant candour of *The Times* and the *New Republic* (though he'd taken issue with its recent pro-Clintonism), which he had once subscribed to, in one of those private moods of exuberance he'd had in America and of whose nature his then-wife had been unaware, in 1992. He had forgotten, last year, for some reason unconnected to his inward, slightly enervating, reappraisal of circumstances, to renew the subscription.

'You can always go to the American Centre,' said his father. 'I don't know if they'll have the—what did you say it was?—the *New Republic*, though.'

Last time he'd been to the American Centre, sceptically, guarding his emigrant status like an undisclosed secret; he was seized not so much by nostalgia as by confusion, and even the Chowringhee outside the glass looked like a photograph. People were turning the pages of newspapers, browsing through videos; *of course* they didn't have the *New Republic*. He'd gone to the toilet; and coming out, had encountered a strange picture comprising three colours, white, yellow, and green, which he hadn't been able to understand. He grew impatient. His mind had been formed by his teachers at school and his father's world, which in turn had been shaped by the late-colonial world (although his father had been against Empire, and was among the ratings who'd sympathized with the three accused of the INA and brought the

Empire down by throwing down their arms). It was a mind that had little tolerance for ambiguity; each time it looked at things, it also looked into the mirror of certainties that had shaped it. Yet when the time had come for Jayojit to choose between Britain and America, he'd chosen the latter; though he never felt it was quite good enough for him. Even the other day, when he'd caught his parents returning from their walk early in the morning, he'd said: 'How quaint of you two!' Explaining, he'd continued, 'You know, in the States, no one walks any more. They drive; and once a week, when they want exercise, they go to the gym.'

'What if they need—need some matches—or milk?' asked his mother, smiling in puzzlement.

Worked up like the boy he once used to be, he said: 'Oh, they phone! Home delivery! And then they go for a "work-out" and walk for hours on a treadmill.'

'But why?' asked the Admiral, trying to piece the jigsaw together.

Jayojit laughed and said: 'They don't want to be alone.'

He headed for the lift in the afternoon; he'd woken from a nap; he couldn't see Bonny anywhere.

There was much less light in that corridor that went straight to the other end of this block; at the end of it was framed, as in a painting, a door with a lock on it. There was a staircase going up and down this way, and another staircase rising at the other end of the long corridor; a window at the staircase landing, and one at the other side, and it was light from these that filled the corridor.

On both sides of the corridor there were three flats; from here, behind the doors, he'd heard the sound of videos and, once, of a music lesson in progress.

He might have come out to smoke a cigarette, but the anti-smoking campaign had got through to him, not so much because of fear but a belated sense of morality; he did not smoke—he had given it up ten years ago.

Most of the residents of these flats—these ones before him—weren't Bengali. They'd tried to make a cheerful go of it, the way settlers bring with them the sense of space that belongs to another culture, two potted plants like insignia outside one of the doors, with lavish leaves; hard to know how they, the plants, made do with so little light. Another door had collapsible gates before it, which meant that, ordinary-looking though the flat might be from the outside, its occupant was far more well-to-do than the Admiral, and possibly had undeclared cash inside; or probably it was ancestral jewellery. The smell of Rajasthani cooking, intimate to strangers, hovered in the corridor here. Another door, at this end of the corridor, had been left inadvertently open, as if suggesting that passers-by were welcome—and in all possibility guests kept coming in all day, and children too kept the door open as they rushed out into the corridor; but the next flat, with a dining table, like the skeleton of some maritime vessel, at the centre, and a tricycle Jayojit could see abandoned by the door, which too had been left open, was barred by an iron gate.

The lift hadn't arrived yet. And there was that humidity that made life difficult just before the monsoons. As Jayojit stood there indecisively, the edges of his spectacles already beginning to steam over, not certain if he should go back, he glimpsed, at the other end of the corridor, a movement he thought he recognized. It was someone he'd come to know from previous visits, the man who looked at his father occasionally, Dr Sen. He'd just arrived on the landing of the fourth storey. He lived in this building, on the eighth floor. Last time had been a time not only of emotional upheaval but of minor illnesses—Jayojit had had a stomach infection, and the Admiral had had high blood pressure. Jayojit's mother had the hardest time of all, because she'd been in perfect health. At that time, Dr Sen had come to the flat a few times, refusing to take, to Jayojit's disbelief, more than fifty rupees per visit—these days, when it was rumoured that doctors in Calcutta charged two hundred rupees for making calls at home!

He had once lived in London in 'digs' when studying for his M.R.C.P. exams: but this whole matter of being a doctor he'd come to take in a disinterested spirit. He was never surprised by an illness, and even when writing out a prescription would be quick to go on to talk about other things—the present Marxist government was one of the 'other things' that kept cropping up—at whose expense he made some tentative but effective jokes. Jayojit saw him as something of a Bengali gentleman, the *bhadralok* and healer personified. He had said:

'I didn't know there were any Bengalis left in the building!'

'You know Bengalis,' the doctor had said in his shy, lambent diction, 'they only come out during the Pujas. Then you'll see them—heh, heh—bowing before Ma Durga! Others, of course, l-like y-you, live abroad, and keep the flats locked up, or give out the flats to Marwaris. Most of the Marwaris are tenants.' He had shaken his head and made a softly uttered judgement. 'It's spoiling the building.' What he meant exactly he hadn't clarified.

They had continued to refer to each other in the formal way, as 'aapni' rather than 'tumi', for the first month they'd known each other, until Jayojit interjected, 'I may be a father and I may have been a husband, but really, I'm much younger than you.' After the second meeting, he'd told the doctor about his divorce, the court case, how he'd refused to recognize the verdict and brought the matter to India; and Dr Sen had listened with proper astonishment and sympathy, as if he could not believe that these things, which he'd only remotely heard about, could actually happen to real people; people with minor complaints like colds, who had fathers who were ageing and stubborn. Part of his surprise was that Jayojit should be the incarnation of this breakdown; such a fine 'boy', educated abroad, obviously doing well in America, earning a sizeable amount in dollars, a person who should be eminently desirable, a 'catch', not a divorcee. Despite the gap in their age of sixteen years, they'd had long conversations and had come to exchange confidences about their respective problems. He'd even known the second girl's family—Arundhati, with whom his parents wanted to set up something. 'I—I'll put in a good word,' he'd said, smiling but quite serious. 'No, no that family's a good one, known them for years.' Then, when things hadn't worked out in the end, 'Please, don't misunderstand ... but I *heard*,' emphasizing that word, as if he'd picked up the information in the air, 'I may be wrong, they said the man wants not a wife as much as a governess to look after his child …' Then silence, a silence that explained more things than actions could. 'But are things all right now?' Dr Sen had asked, ruminating, that summer.

'Things can never be all *right,* I guess,' Jayojit had said, 'but my son will be with me for at least part of the year.' Had Jayojit imagined it, or had the doctor, since then, spoken to him with a special gentleness? But no one's life is perfect; the doctor himself was involved in a litigation with his brother, a property dispute: it had been going on for years. Saddened, he now wanted to end the dispute and let his brother have the property, which was somewhere on the outskirts of Calcutta. 'Keep it, I want to say to him,' he'd told Jayojit, almost wearily, reminiscently. 'I don't want it.' Yet the doctor had achieved a sort of composure by taking regular walks and keeping to a strict diet; 'Exercise is important,' he'd said in some context during a visit.

'Dr Sen!'

The figure, about to descend the flight of stairs, looked vaguely in Jayojit's direction.

Jayojit found himself walking fast towards him, down the corridor he'd been looking at absently so far. He moved quickly but heavily—because of the heat, and the excess weight he'd gained in the last few months.

'Dr Sen!' he repeated, coming closer.

The doctor didn't respond at first, but as Jayojit came nearer, recognition came.

'What a surprise!' he said, smiling. Then, 'Jayojit! A-are you well? When did you come back?'

The same soft, almost liquid way of speaking.

'It's been about three weeks—a month,' said Jayojit, thinking back briefly. 'But tell me, Dr Sen, how are you?'

'Strange …' said the doctor, musing seriously. 'I haven't seen you …' Then a smile returned to his face as unexpectedly. 'Well, things go on. Nothing to report from here,' he laughed gently, using the English word 'report' in his sentence. A black crow, oddly majestic, alighted at the window of the lower landing.

The doctor was wearing a greyish-green t-shirt and trousers—there had evidently been no change in his appearance in these past nine months. He was balding, but looked much younger than his fifty-six years; for he had a light, quick stride—unlike, for instance, Jayojit's father, who ambled heavily. It must be his regular exercises, his long walks in the compound and down the lane (he always walked alone, never with his wife) that kept him trim. In many ways, in fact, he led a bachelor's life (it was difficult to catch a glimpse of Mrs Sen). The spectacles he wore did not succeed in giving him a focused look, but dispersed the direction of his gaze. He was about four inches shorter than Jayojit—who wondered, for an instant, how the doctor's court case was going.

'Heh—I got tired of waiting for the lift,' said the doctor with a chuckle, as if he felt the need to explain, now that he'd been seen doing it, the purpose of embarking on this unusual adventure of going down eight flights of stairs. 'But one can't do this all the time.' A man of great energy, apparently, something belied by the slowness of his speech. Then:

'But you're quite well, I trust? No stomach infections?' he smiled. 'Thank God! No, I say this only because of this nasty weather, cool under the fan, hot outside, the change of season coming,' again, the words 'change of season' in English; he shook his head in a grim, condoling way, as if speaking of a regrettable political manoeuvre. '*Lots* of diseases this time of the year,' he said, 'viral fevers, gastro-intestinal problems,' the doctor for the first time ventriloquizing unselfconsciously through him as he uttered the terms, 'bacterial infections, influenza.'

'Then you must be very busy,' said Jayojit.

'No, no! ... I mainly lecture at the medical college these days,' said the doctor, as if a subtle gear had shifted within him. 'I go to the hospital once a week, and I see the patients who call me.' He meant that he no longer sat at a chamber. Behind the doctor's seemingly fluid lifestyle, some sort of choice had been exercised; at some point he'd taken the decision that making money would take on a secondary importance in his life.

'How is your father?' asked Dr Sen, looking up and, for the first time, meeting Jayojit's gaze. 'I don't think it's time to do an ECG again, is it? Anyway,' he waved his hand, 'we can talk of those things later. How long will *you* be here?'

'Till the end of June, most probably. Or early July,' said Jayojit, as if he lived in a time when the simplest things were subject to unresolvable influences. 'That'll leave me about a month to the end of July, when my college leave ends and, anyway, when I have to take my son back.'

'Hu—hu,' said the doctor, before Jayojit had even completed the sentence, like one absent-mindedly soothing a child or allaying an agitation within himself. 'He must be taller now …' referring to the boy—then, delightedly, as if he had quite forgotten, and as if no personal calamity could take away this simple, happy fact: 'They grow so quickly at this age, don't they!' A little hesitantly, 'Uh—Vikram, isn't it? Or is it Benoy?'

'Vikram—that's his proper name,' said Jayojit. 'But we call him Bonny at home.'

'Bonny!' laughed Dr Sen, that unfocused look returning. He gazed downward at the floor. *'Bonny.* Yes … yes …' He seemed to be remembering something. Then he looked up at the space above the staircase and said without real interest: 'Any plans—going anywhere?'

'Not really. I'm planning to complete—no,' he laughed, 'begin, I should say—my second book,' said Jayojit. 'I don't write quickly …'—this was confessed with regret—'I take a while. I hope it will deal with the ethics of developmental policy.'

'Very good. Excellent,' said Dr Sen, nodding. 'Economists are doing well these days, aren't they? In my days it was Professor Amiya Dasgupta and …' he hummed, 'Bhabatosh Dutta! My word, all the students swore by him.' Jayojit waited patiently, as a 'modern' composer might preserve a decorous silence as Beethoven is praised. 'I think Amartya might have been his student … Amartya Sen … My God, he's done well! When d'you think he'll get the Nobel Prize—or do you think he'll get it?'

'It depends on which political lobby is currently dominant,' said Jayojit with a laugh, but feeling an unpleasant weight too at having to speculate on another's career. He was a generation younger than Sen, but felt equal to him; there were others equal to him; and yet he was defined by him as well. 'It's more politics than anything else. I mean also which school of thought exercises most power at the moment. Whether it's free-market friendly or not.'

'Is that so ... is that so ...' The doctor shook his head. Then he brightened and said, 'Yes, that *is* so, isn't it? They didn't give it to Gandhi but they gave it to Kissinger!' he said, indignant, as if he'd been in the midst of those events. 'I used to know him, you know, not very well, of course, when I was a student.' Jayojit was perplexed. 'Where does he teach now (I've heard his marriages haven't lasted)?' and he realized it was Amartya Sen he was talking about. 'We're about the same age, you know ...'

'Harvard, I think. Though he seems to be everywhere at once ... In Oxford, in Cambridge, tomorrow at Jadavpur.'

They pondered briefly on how human beings at times seemed no more substantial than rumours. Suddenly, in an aside: 'America's one country I've never been to.'

'I don't know if you've missed much. You must have seen Americans here—they go everywhere! Well, if you've seen one—' Interrupting himself, Jayojit thought back and said, 'It's warm there now: some places are even hotter than here.'

'I have some nieces and nephews there,' said Dr Sen. 'One in New York, another in a place called Mon Montana.'

Jayojit narrowed his eyes, wondering if he might possibly know the people the doctor had mentioned. 'Mm,' he said. 'Big

Sky country,' he concluded emphatically. 'Montana—they have a bright blue sky out there. Emptiness.'

'My nephew's a general surgeon there,' the doctor continued, incurious about what Jayojit thought of the vistas of the American interior. He glanced swiftly at his wristwatch and said: 'A-are you about to go down—going out, maybe?'

'I was thinking of it,' said Jayojit. 'It's a bit hot, isn't it?'

Dr Sen smiled sadly and shook his head, as if at a regrettable piece of news which had only just been revealed to him. 'It's *terribly* hot!' They began to go down the stairs.

Jayojit and Amala had married eleven years ago; eleven years and seven months precisely. That was when that evening pleasantness had set in, the month of Hemanta on the Bengali calendar. They had been divorced at the end of the year before last in a bright, clean Midwestern summer. It hadn't been an easy or even a civilized event; the court had ruled that Amala, who'd taken the child with her, would have full custody. His first reaction was that all was lost. Then he'd decided he must fight; not just his studied determination but his natural belligerence had guided him. He employed a new lawyer; 'I'm sorry, Gary, but I have to think of other eventualities,' he'd said to the old one on the phone.

Hundreds of miles away, the Admiral quickly grasped the legal niceties. Examining the loopholes and details helped to lift him from the depression that he felt at almost all times during that period.

'But can it be done, though?' the Admiral had asked over the telephone at well past midnight—meaning moving the case to the Indian courts.

'Why not?' Jayojit had asked, out of breath with agitation.

Their child was gone; six miles away, but further away than India. 'If it hasn't been done it will be now.' Pause; the roar of the long-distance line that swallowed voices and sometimes sent them back. 'I'm an Indian citizen, aren't I?'

Another deliberate pause; because if you interrupted the speaker the words cancelled each other out. You had to be sure the other person had finished. Sometimes there was an echo.

'But Bonny's not,' the Admiral offered. 'He's not, is he?'

'He's too small to be any kind of citizen,' Jayojit had said. 'Anyway, we're not talking about the son here, but the father. The father's prerogative.'

It was at that time, the Admiral remembered, that the question of what it was to be an 'Indian' had had to be addressed. It was not something that either Jayojit or Admiral Chatterjee had bothered about, except during moments of political crisis or significance, like a border conflict or elections, or some moment of mass celebration, when it seemed all right to mock 'Indianness', if only to differentiate oneself from a throng of people; but this was a legal matter.

'We're going to go to Gariahat,' he said to Bonny. The boy was in the toilet; he ran out, attempting determinedly to fit a button into his shorts' buttonhole. It was their third trip to that place; each time Jayojit found an appropriate reason.

Last year he'd savoured, in the humidity of the late and vanishing monsoons, some of the smoking foods on the pavements. The reason he'd been experimental was because the food was fried; and it had settled lightly in his stomach and left him unscathed; and left no imprint on the surface of his mind.

Jayojit's mother was worried.

'How will you go?' she asked; her face recorded her unhappiness. This, despite the fact that he'd been there six days ago on a private misadventure.

'Oh, I'm *sure* we'll find a way,' said Jayojit, tying his shoelaces.

'Don't take the bus, baba,' said his mother; as if she were advising against needless self-endangerment. 'Whatever you do.'

'No chance of that—don't worry.'

The Admiral, as if he'd overheard, came out of the bedroom and said:

'I can give you the keys to the car.' This was uttered as if it were a startling, slightly embarrassing, confession. 'It's a bit old, but the Fiat's an excellent car—doesn't have the Ambassador's reputation for sturdiness, but it's actually much sturdier. I'm not sure if it's got enough petrol though.' The Fiat had been acquired cheap before retirement; and its engine had vibrated mildly until it had arrived at its state of voluntary repose, when its windows were cleaned twice a week from the outside.

Last time Jayojit had just walked; now his father stood before him, undecided.

'Ha!' he said, waving one hand, declaiming to the balcony. 'No thank you! No, I don't think I'm quite ready to take on the Calcutta traffic …'

Something in his father's tone caught Bonny's attention; he stopped to watch him with large eyes.

'It's much better there, isn't it?' said the Admiral.

Only one place was referred to as *there* these days; but at one time it used to be the Admiral's in-laws' home.

'In general,' said Jayojit, his voice louder than usual. But his old cynicism about America soon got the better of him, and he felt unable to commend any of its virtues without causing discomfort to a part of himself; he added, 'If you don't get run into from behind by some schizophrenic motorist.'

In the lane, Bonny ran a little way ahead ('Careful!' said his father). A watchman said: 'Kahaa jate ho, baba?'; he knew Bonny now, but received no acknowledgement in return except an increase in speed. Raat-ki-rani and nameless but characteristic creepers, a colony whose presence was taken for granted, flourished by the gate. He didn't always obey everything his father said; it was Amala who used to be the symbol of authority at home, and the one who would invariably dispense it. Nothing that had happened yet had changed the way that he viewed his parents; he saw the present arrangement as an experiment. He couldn't clearly distinguish between fifteen minutes and half an hour, let alone knowing what a longer period of time was.

'That's a pretty big house,' said Bonny after his father had caught up with him, standing suddenly to look at a two-storeyed mansion, probably built in the twenties or thirties, repainted yellow. A banyan stood alone in the courtyard, and its shadow sat meditating beneath it. 'Is the guy who owns it quite rich?'

There was an outbreak of shrill chattering in the branches. The slatted windows of the mansion looked back blankly at the boy.

'Might have been at one time,' said Jayojit. 'Probably gone mad by now, all alone in that huge place.' There was no sound; the birds were quiet again. 'Yeah; right,' said the boy.

Yet something had made him pause before the old house, not just because of its largeness, but its silence in the midst of all the small sounds.

'There's a taxi,' said Jayojit, pointing to a shadow. Abruptly, as if he'd become aware of the sunlight between the trees, Bonny narrowed his eyes. Then he looked at the taxi; last time they'd walked to Gariahat.

Jayojit's mother had once told him, 'Joy, there's always a taxi at the corner of the lane'; now her words came back to him.

Two men, in their late twenties or early thirties, were sitting on the front seat, a geometry of detachment. The heat was like a presence in the taxi; one could sense it from outside. Jayojit knocked twice on the door at the back.

'Will you go?' he asked, bending forward. The driver turned to look at him. 'Kahaa?' he asked, avoiding his eye.

'Gariahat.'

A pause; then the driver shook his head, and his companion shifted slightly.

'Bloody fool,' thought Jayojit, his silent but vehement voice surprising himself, and then gently steered Bonny towards the main road.

Some of the trees were still heavy with gulmohur blossoms. At intervals in the lane, they recurred, the ones in the distance a blurred mass of deep orange. They found a taxi on the main road going in the other direction.

'Gariahat?' said Jayojit, uncharacteristically tentative now; more tense than tentative. He'd lost the knack of talking to these people and it often made him rude. Light shimmered upon the doors of the taxi. The driver, older than him or approximately his age, gestured to the back, and leaned forward to swing down the meter; Bonny, entering, sat at the edge and rested his chin disconsolately on the shiny plastic of the front seat.

'The market,' Jayojit said in Bengali, loudly, as if he were speaking in a foreign language.

The taxi moved slowly; Bonny's head vibrating gently with the motion.

On the way they passed, at intervals, two ice-cream carts pushed by men in blue uniforms who almost immediately became reflections in the driver's mirror.

'What's Kwality?' asked Bonny.

Meanwhile, the driver, all of a sudden animated, blew his horn at a slow-moving private car, driven by an old man before him.

'What's Kwality?'

After a couple of repetitions, Jayojit said: 'Oh, "quality"! Let's see … that's the *value* of a thing. How good or bad a thing is.'

'Oh,' said Bonny. As Jayojit began thinking to himself about the way everyday speech had entered the language of economics and vice versa—for instance, the word 'value'—Bonny said, 'Why's it painted on those vans?'

'What is?'

'Kwality,' came the reply.

A moment later, illumination came. 'Oh that's the name of an *ice-cream,*' he said. He realized that he had become something of a pedant with his son, always doing his best to rescue him from spelling mistakes and misinformation; unrepentant, he said, 'That's not a real word! The word *I* was talking about is'—and he spelt 'quality'.

'Ice-cream?' said Bonny, lifting his chin from the seat, as if, like doughnuts, ice-cream was too outrageous to mention here.

'You can have some later,' promised Jayojit. This was a commitment to be honoured at some unspecified moment. 'Can I have some now, baba?' asked Bonny, tilting his face into the shadow, towards his father.

'Not *now,* Bonny, sorry,' said Jayojit, slapping a housefly off his trousers, and then busily smoothing them again. 'See, the ice-cream van's *gone*'—his voice shook as the taxi tried to swerve unsuccessfully around a pothole—'and ...' He left the sentence unfinished, as if he'd already conveyed what he wanted to say. As an afterthought, he said, *'Gariahat* might have ice-cream.'

Just outside, the sun lay like fire on the pavement; two peasants sat on their haunches upon a kerb.

There were children everywhere, scattered and released from school; a pavement stall selling newspapers.

They were approaching the market; the tramlines here met and gleamed.

'Turn left and stop there,' said Jayojit, pointing to the opposite side of the road.

They waited for a tram to pass, the taxi already tensed to

compete with a neighbouring car to make the first movement. When the taxi jerked forward, Bonny clutched the seat with his fingers, puzzled, but the impulse to race was spent almost as soon as it was surrendered to, and they were no more in motion.

'How much?' Jayojit asked, opening the door and stepping out. 'Careful, Bonny, don't get out on that side'; afraid because of the buses like juggernauts.

The meter said nine rupees.

'Tero taka,' said the driver. Thirteen rupees; lucky number. Jayojit took out the notes from his wallet and handed them to the driver—they were from the second wad of cash he'd got across the counter after coming here, and the perforations from where the staples had been violently prised open still showed—who counted them, and fished in his pocket for change. There seemed to be confusion about whether, indeed, the driver had the change or not.

'Fourteen, fifteen,' he said finally, as if muttering a charm to the counting of a rupee and two fifty paisa coins, and completed the transaction by dropping them into Jayojit's palm.

He turned and found that Bonny wasn't there. Where in the world is he? He went through the narrow passage between two stalls, and saw a boy in a t-shirt standing before a shop: Bonny.

'Ei khokababu,' said a voice, 'ei khokababu!'

'Don't disappear like that,' said Jayojit to the unsurprised boy. 'OK?'

Bonny assented by saying nothing and lifting his eyes to look at his father; then he rubbed one eye with the back of a hand.

'Dada—take a look at these shirts!'

Bonny was wearing sneakers; he must be hot—it might be an idea to buy him a pair of sandals. Where was Bata?

They went past vendors selling fruit on beds of straw.Mangoes had just come into season, piled pale green on baskets, but theirs was a peculiar family, because the Admiral couldn't stand mangoes and the mess they made, and Jayojit had inherited his father's fastidiousness; his mother, over the last few years, had become stoic; and the money she thus saved compensated somewhat for her yearning for the first langra and himsagar. Finally, Jayojit paused and went inside a store and asked for Dove soap. His mother had said 'Dove' wistfully when he'd asked her which soap they used these days; it used to be Pears, he knew, but on this visit, like a new discovery, it was Dove; and since it was more expensive, a rare indulgence. As if by coincidence, he now saw an advertisement on one of the glass windows of the cabinets inside. The model, in the make-believe opulence of her bath, looked familiar, but she couldn't be, she was too young; he'd stopped noticing models for years now; the last model he could remember—and he was surprised at the trivial information his mind retained—was called Anne Bredemeyer. 'Dove,' he said, without knowing who would respond; there were three men behind the counter who themselves had the searching air of visitors.

'Give us a Dove soap!' said a man in kurta and pyjamas to someone at the back, then turned to Jayojit, 'Anything else?'

Jayojit looked at the medicine racks behind the man, looking back at Bonny to see if he was on the steps, noted the fan overhead, and scanned the shelves for shampoo. But it was conditioner he wanted; his hair was greying; the grey had been seeping into the black. But he didn't see any conditioner, unless it was disguised as something else; he saw bottles that said 'frequent use' and 'for greasy hair'. His hair, if anything, was too dry. About five or more seconds had passed since the thin man had said 'Aar kichhu?'— and now Jayojit found himself saying, 'Colgate toothpaste achhe?' almost ironically, then pondering on a suitable reply to 'Chhoto na bado?'—'Small or large?'; and as an afterthought, adding 'talcum powder'.

He'd seen a commercial on television the day before yesterday in which a busybody of a child was brushing his teeth with Colgate.

'Which powder?' asked the man behind the counter, who was shrunken but fastidious.

'Any will do,' confessed Jayojit. 'Pond's,' he said; the word had just come to him out of nowhere.

'Pond's,' the man said. He turned. 'Jodu,' he called, 'Pond's talcum powder de!'

Another man came out from behind a cupboard and looked at Jayojit with the interested equanimity of one looking at himself in a mirror.

'Pond's?' he said, as if he was not sure if he'd heard correctly, and retreated again.

More fumblings.

'That's seventy rupees,' said the man at last, writing numbers secretively on the back of an envelope.

On the way back they stopped at a bookshop that Jayojit noticed behind a photocopying and STD booth. The sky had darkened a few minutes before they entered. The man who ran the shop, dressed in a creased dhoti and kurta, regarded the rain without wonder or accusation as it began to fall in isolated drops.

'Baba, I wanna touch it,' cried Bonny, jumping in the doorway by the bookshelves.

'Go on then.'

The shopkeeper looked up once again—as if at a noise in the distance—and looked downward. The lane was subsumed in a gloom which made the colours of the unremarkable multistoreyed building before them more visible. 'But the rains aren't supposed to start till two weeks later,' thought Jayojit, irritated, thinking of the weather fronts and insubstantial bands of high pressure building up over the South and the coasts of Kerala; grateful, too, for the breeze. Contemptuous, he turned his back to the drama of the rains. He looked, unseeing, at the rows of Penguin Indias, and registered, remotely, as one would the words of an exotic language, the Marquezes, Vargas Llosas; next to them, slim books of horoscopes; arranged for a reader who wasn't very clear about what he was looking for.

He began to look for a book at random; noted the motto 'Everyman, I will be thy guide'; stared, with some scepticism, at some of the books by Indian writers; 'They not only look light, they feel lightweight as well,' he thought, weighing one in his hand; he picked up a new paperback of *A Suitable Boy* with a theatrical air which there was no one to note. The last book he'd read was a volume treading, in the fog of post-structuralist theory, a tightrope between history and Keynesian economics; and he was going to give it a bad review for the university humanities journal. A colleague, an Italian American called Antonio who edited the journal, had sent it to him with a note: 'Dear J, I know there are worse things in life than reading a deconstruction of classical economic theory (tell me about it!) but things aren't half as bad as you think. Snap out of it, pal, and send me 1,500 words when you feel like it. Don't leave it till the millennium. Best, Tony.' Antonio, settled with three children, married to a half-Vietnamese, half-French American, setting up the book for a bad review, knowing full well Jayojit's distaste for airy-fairy 'theory'. But Bonny was getting his t-shirt damp with the spray. Afraid of being reprimanded by his mother (he feared not so much his mother's words as her silences), Jayojit said:

'Come in here, you!'

'Oh, baba!'

He hopped into the shop, throwing a glance at the books stacked everywhere. Jayojit brushed the moisture from the boy's hair with his fingers. 'Stand still!' Then: 'Turn round'; the boy turning not so much obediently as displaying his swiftness; yet the tiniest bit afraid of his father's brusqueness. 'OK.' He was thin now with burnt-up energy, but when he'd been born he'd been seven and a half pounds and his grandmother, his mother's mother, had said, after the long night: 'Ki bonny baby eta!' Yes, Bonny had been pink ('a little white mouse', his mother had called him), with a hint of black hair which Amala repeatedly admired. They'd been in Claremont then, the nursing home had been on the outskirts, and the grandmother had come to be with her daughter. A week later, when it had come home, Jayojit had taken footage of the child, its first movements in the cot between the double bed and cupboard, and moments captured from its spells of sleep, on a camcorder, dipping into the baby's life with the lens for two days, and then made videos for both sets of parents, who'd noted both the baby and the beauty of the house. The shopkeeper seemed not to notice the boy and the thirty-seven-year-old father's exchange; keeping a vigil, he stared at Jayojit, his eyelids flickered respectfully, and, after opening his mouth to yawn, turned back to the books he was stacking on the table.

'How much is this?' asked Jayojit. He was holding a large hardcover in one hand; the picture of a cheetah, gold and black, jumped out of the cover. Its shadow leapt with the lightning.

The shopkeeper touched the book as if he intended, by some power of transformation, to make it seem like a saleable commodity. Wrapped in cellophane, its price was scribbled on the first page. 'Five hundred and twenty rupees,' he said; some of his teeth were rust-brown with betel. His eyes held Jayojit's. 'Hm.' Jayojit turned the pages and consulted them heavy-handedly, superiorly. 'Well, less than what I'd pay for it in New York,' he thought.

The next morning, the first day of the last week of May, he woke up feeling vulnerable and exposed. He hadn't felt desire in a long time. Bonny'd been born, and at that time there had been a cutting off of sexual activity. Instead, when they had time, they would go to parks and sit on benches, admire the Fall's redness that hung about the trees like an aura, talk about the new General Electric factory that was to come up in the outskirts and what it would do to jobs and to Claremont, and discuss moving to big cities in the East.

'When I was a kid, you know,' he told her when they were talking about the appeal of New York, and the fact that New York is attractive to every kind of Indian, from taxi drivers to dentists, 'I used to think the Big Apple was the studio where the Beatles recorded their songs.'

She, in turn, warming to her memory of the Beatles, revealed to him how she'd liked Paul the best of the four, and how her friends would count how old they'd be when he was thirty-five. '*I'm* twenty-nine now,' she said, watching two children play with a frisbee. 'He must be ... forty-five.'

'You'll still be quite young when he's sixty-four,' said Jayojit.

She turned to him in mock disdain. 'Poor joke, Mr Chatterjee,' she said.

'I'm a Lennon fan myself,' he'd said, remembering the sixties in which both he and Amala had grown up, she in Calcutta and he in so many different places.

He lay there, thinking of what he'd dreamed of, and couldn't return to it. Had he had indigestion? A crow perched on the silent air-conditioner was crying out repeatedly. He gave himself to recalling, for a couple of minutes, what it was that accounted for this pressure of longing; as if it were someone else's body, he discovered he had an erection beneath his shorts. He was bare-chested—he'd taken off his shirt during a power-cut in the morning—and his body-hair was ink-black spread against the fair skin.

He got up to urinate; washed his face; glanced at the watch; nine forty-five. It had rained when they were sleeping, a stealthy downpour; the water from the tap was cool. They might have had another child. Two to five minutes, that's all it took. In retrospect, thank God they didn't.

He didn't dry his face immediately, but draped the towel around his neck, his forehead moist.

His mother was standing near the dining table.

'Once the rains come'—to her, evidently, the incontrovertible fact of rainfall wasn't enough; the rains would only 'come' when it was time for them to, the 10th of June—'I'll have to dry these in the bathroom,' she said, looking at the clothes in the verandah.

'Why don't you buy a washing machine?'

His mother looked up. 'Joy, they have new ones in that shop in Gariahat—"Pleasant"—I've seen them; they wring the clothes so dry that it takes only half a day to dry them.'

'I know,' said Jayojit, with the air of speaking of a celebrated personality with whom he was already on first-name terms. 'Who makes them?' he asked.

'There's that one,' she said vaguely, 'BPL ... No—IBF or IFB ...' She sounded tired and unconvinced.

There was a difference between his parents with regard to appliances; his father distrusted them as he would a rival; his mother had no confidence in using them, but none the less desired them. There was no doubt that a washing machine would help; probably it was too expensive for them. Jayojit wondered if he could offer to buy them one.

'But what use will it be?' said the Admiral, dismissing the idea with a wave of one hand.

Mrs Chatterjee would say nothing; she would not argue with her husband.

'They've been around in the US for more than fifty years now,' said Jayojit, slightly impatient. 'They don't seem to have done too badly—so I presume they have *some* uses.'

'But we have *cheap labour,* Joy,' said Admiral Chatterjee, as if making an important point.

'Once, being married was to have cheap labour,' said Jayojit. A little coldly, he added, 'That was a joke.'

'You know what I mean,' said his father, still pursuing his original line of thought. 'You know what I'm saying. It's easier—and cheaper—to have what's-her-name do the washing than to buy a washing machine.' He said, 'Even if they sold these things in the Fort William canteen'—referring to the place where the Armed Forces could buy certain things at a reduced price—'which I doubt they do, it would still be dear.'

The sharp conversation reminded Mrs Chatterjee of her husband's working days and of the time of her own relative youth. But she enjoyed the impassioned exchange between father and son, the language giving it an intimacy which they could only communicate to each other in words which not so much excluded her as turned her into a spectator.

'That's not a worry. If buying it's the worrisome bit, there's nothing to worry. Because I'm thinking of buying it.'

The Admiral stared at him, absorbing this final bit of information, this decision that had been taken without him.

'This is your doing,' he said, turning to his wife. 'Tumi ki bolechho oke?' The accusing Bengali words sounded as unconfrontational as flute-music. For the first time in what seemed a while, Mrs Chatterjee allowed herself a smile.

'She hasn't told me anything, baba! It's my idea. The way you're reacting is as if the washing machine was some suspect foreign gadget that arrived here yesterday. You know, it's been around for more than ten years.'

The Admiral became glum, like a child always used to having his own way finding himself again in a situation where all is not going as he wishes it to.

'It's out of the question. Besides, I don't think it's a good idea.'

Jayojit sighed. It was difficult to negotiate with his father when he was in this dogmatic mood.

'We're living in a consumer society, baba,' said Jayojit. 'We might as well make use of it.' So saying, he suddenly unbuttoned the top of his shirt and began to fan himself with an old magazine.

'We are … we are,' said the Admiral, not sounding very pleased, as if the realization had dawned on him in a moment of final and unexpected insight.

'I need a glass of water,' said Jayojit, getting up abruptly. 'My throat keeps going dry in this heat.'

'Not just one glass, baba!' said his mother. 'You must have at least eight glasses a day, isn't it?' She looked around, beaming. 'And the same is true,' she said, 'for a young man I know.'

Heat, cold, heat, cold … especially when the air-conditioner was switched on. And the Admiral, having gone in once to convey some message to Jayojit, had stepped out into a wall of heat.

'This is not good for anyone,' he'd said. 'This is why I don't like this city. This swamp climate and that artificial coolness.' He scratched his beard. And though the city was the Admiral's birthplace, he didn't feel it was; he was always a newcomer here, slightly taken aback by the weather and the people.

No wonder, then, that Bonny sneezed once or twice a couple of days later; he wasn't used to sneezing; it made him feel slightly conspicuous.

'What's this, what's this, when did this happen?' said Jayojit, showing his teeth in a smile.

The Admiral looked displeased, as if he'd contracted a cold himself.

'"Running nose" ache?' called Bonny's grandmother from a distance, sounding concerned and professional.

'Let's see if you have a runny nose, pal,' said Jayojit, getting up from the sofa. The light of the laptop he'd sat facing for the last forty-five minutes went off. 'No, it's f-i-ine,' reassured Jayojit, scrutinizing the boy's face. 'It's a little moist, but it's all right, really.'

He took his son to the museum that afternoon, and before the exhibits Bonny sneezed embarrassedly three or four times, and was at a loss to understand the beauty of Gandhara sculpture. Instead, he stared at an American couple in shorts, craning forward to examine a Buddha; they were something he could recognize. All the Buddhas were in meditation; half-smiling, they'd transcended the trauma of that first registering of disease, old age, and death with which the quest had begun; while Bonny peered at a card and said: 'B.C. Hey, that's Before Christ, baba!'

Outside, in spite of the runny nose, they had ice-cream, Bonny a vanilla cone, Jayojit an orange stick.

And returning, Jayojit told the Admiral without much amusement:

'The most interesting relic was the museum itself.'

Late that night, a blocked nose developed, and Jayojit, listening to Bonny's breathing, had half a mind to switch off the run-down air-conditioning. When he went to the bathroom, the heat was disturbed by a flash of lightning, and then the sound of thunder. Jayojit experienced a stirring within him even as he tied the cords of his pyjamas.

Returning, he saw his son was breathing with his mouth

open. He felt his forehead to see if it was warm; held his hand against his own forehead to see which was warmer; there was a flash of lightning outside the window. The boy had no temperature.

Without his spectacles Jayojit looked blank; and he needed to take them off—a heavy tortoise-shell frame—and wipe them. But now it had begun to rain more frequently. Before it rained there was a breeze to herald the coming downpour. And this was making Jayojit sing:

Da da da da nai chini go she ki
Turu tu tu turu turu

That morning he read an editorial in a damp newspaper about how economic liberalization was urgently required, but how, too, if introduced without caution, it might lead not only to the loss of what was seen to be Indian culture, but to uncontrollable economic disparity.

Do we want to go the way of Brazil or South Korea? The former's economic 'progress' has been unstable to say the least, and darkened by undesirable social problems, while the latter has only consolidated itself. As Prof. Sen has pointed out, this consolidation is related to the successful campaigns for literacy and healthcare in that country: India must learn from this. The problem we face with liberalization is not, after all, the loss of our culture and native traditions. For what is Indian culture, anyway? It has been redefined at every stage in history by its contact with what at first was perceived as 'foreign'. No, the problem is whether India can provide the basic infrastructure—not only industrial infrastructure, but the infrastructure of human resources—that can not only benefit from but contribute to liberalization.

'What are you reading?' asked the Admiral, hovering about his son. Since the weather had cooled he had become more energetic.

'I suppose it's not uninteresting,' said Jayojit. 'But mixed up. The eternal question: the chicken or the egg.'

Jayojit had had a dream while in university, like his fellow students, about socialism and a just world order; but no longer; now the important questions were whether there could be justice without economic well-being, whether, in a poor country, healthcare and literacy needed to be a prerequisite to deregulation, or whether deregulation would provide the economic wherewithal for literacy and healthcare.

Di di di nai chini go she ki
… Jani ne, jani ne

Later that afternoon, he even wondered if he should write the *Statesman* a letter; leisure had slowed down his thoughts, and he'd been too long away from the lecturing mode; like a teething child, faintly despondent, he needed to bite into something. He even had a sentence running in his head with which to begin: 'Sir, with reference to your article in the leader, one must begin by sounding a note of caution about assuming that economic deregulation will be a panacea to all our problems; but it will, no doubt, be one to some of them.' This sentence ran in his head, its shape changing slightly.

He considered putting it down on the computer on the dining-table. When he connected it to a socket, it flashed to life, its light at first hurting his eyes. Peering, he strained to read at a glance the crowd of icons; the cursor moved at his touch. Yet immediately he lost interest in the blank slate of the screen, and noticed that the time on the screen was wrong; it was the time in Claremont; 'Damn thing.'

He went to the apple which had a bit of it chewed off; the arrow settled on it lightly. His mother, on the sofa, was saying:

'Bonny, let me see if you have grown taller.'

'Not now, tamma.'

'Why, what are you doing, shona?'

He was retrieving a toy car that had gone underneath a cupboard.

'I'm *busy*, tamma.' He was never not busy. Even the cold hadn't slowed him down. Yet there were times when he just lay on his back, staring at the ceiling; was it the heat? He breathed deeply as he got up now, and wiped his nose.

'Come here and let me see,' said his grandmother. 'Thhammar

kachhe esho.'

'OK.'

After looking him up and down and nodding, as if she'd been right, Mrs Chatterjee said:

'How old will you be?'

'How old?'

'How old, next year, baba?' Teasing him, she looked at him. Just yesterday, before midday, when she'd closed her eyes for five minutes before the tiny gods and goddesses by the dressing-table, his face had come to her eyes. Sometimes she could see Amala in the boy's straight eyebrows and in his small forehead.

The boy considered this question with gravity. 'Eight,' he said reluctantly.

'When will you be taller than me?' Mrs Chatterjee said. It began to rain. Bonny ran towards the verandah and pressed his face against the grille. 'Wow,' he said.

The Admiral stood in the balcony, allowing the wind to unsettle his hair. He switched on an electric light, and Bonny's shadow fell to his left and enveloped part of the furniture.

'Where's it coming from?' the Admiral said, regarding what could either have been the grille or a point beyond it.

Jayojit had changed the time from 5:32 a.m., in which the colon between the numbers pulsed repeatedly, to 3:32 p.m. by simply moving the band from Detroit, USA, to Calcutta, India. He rubbed an eye; the light from the screen had begun to hurt his eyes ever since the sky'd become dark.

His mother was now removing, rather unhappily, some of the damp clothes from the clothesline.

Kites descended at times as low as this balcony. Then they took off again.

It wasn't clear whether this was simply a seasonal change; though it was true that they hadn't been seen so close during the summer. Their wings hooded their bodies, and Jayojit had gone up quite close to one and noticed how pointed and talon-like its beak was. They usually sat on the parapets outside windows, or on the ends of pipes.

The weather dictated other small changes. Mrs Chatterjee had to move the plants in the verandah (which she appeared to ignore but which, as it turned out, she actually tended to carefully when no one else was around) to the right, where they could get more light. And the clothesline, on which the clothes used to act like weathervanes to the wind and heat, was moved to Jayojit's parents' bathroom.

A few times, of late, the Admiral had found his grandson playing hide-and-seek among the two clotheslines that had been hung in his bathroom. He'd bent to wash his face, and had heard a sound; unbending, he'd say, 'Who's that?' Bonny emerged from behind the drying clothes. 'What's this, dadu,' said the Admiral. 'You're here?' 'You didn't see me at first, did you, dadu?'

'You have a regular garden here,' said Jayojit to his mother, relaxing in the verandah. 'What *are* these plants?'

'Oh, don't ask me,' said Mrs Chatterjee. 'Mali used to

come, but he doesn't come these days. All for the good ...' she pondered. 'I have to pay Maya two hundred rupees, we can't afford another one.' Always exaggerating this state of being hard up, he thought. She turned to look at a plant, as if she'd just noticed it. 'That one's eglonomia; that one,' shifting her gaze, 'is money plant.'

'Nice leaves,' said Jayojit, looking critically at the eglonomia. He tore off part of a leaf—it was dying—with a finicky, calculated movement. The sun dimmed, as if it had been snuffed out, and then kindled again as a cloud moved past.

The 29th of May. A small desk ANZ Readymoney calendar, with photographs of wildlife accompanying each month; it had come as a gift from the bank. Jayojit's mother was choosy about calendars; calendars came and calendars went; there were calendars from steel plants and fledgling joint-ventures that were given away as gifts; this one she had kept on the wall-unit in the living room, next to an old, wooden, miniature tusker that was advancing somewhere, and which would look deprived of purpose without it next to it.

Jayojit had gone out to the American Express office on Old Court House Street, whose façade was dominated by opaque sheets of glass, to change some traveller's cheques, and then passed the Governor's (once the Viceroy's) house on the way back, to the Grindlays Bank in the south, where he had an account. He had opened the account three years ago, not so much on an impulse as guided by instinct, not to speak of fresh opportunities the bank was presenting to NRIs, so that interest rates were not only higher here than in the recession-ridden West, but that, more promisingly, the money could be converted, whenever he wished it, to foreign exchange. They sent him bank statements, of course; and cheque books.

'I waited in the bank for a while—after all, it's air-conditioned—reading all the ads for ANZ Readymoney. I thought, what the hell, it's not pouring too heavily, I'll risk it and take a cab.'

After a while he said, as if admitting to something slightly embarrassing:

'I like that branch.'

The Admiral said:

'Yes, I like it too. And that fellow who works there—Sanyal; Dr Sanyal's son. Always helpful.'

Jayojit, though, when he walked through the glass doors into the air-conditioned space, forgot about Sanyal. Once you came into close contact with the staff, you realized that things were being run with some tardiness and confusion; not confusion, perhaps, but something like it. Jayojit disliked being ignored for too long; he realized, wryly, that he had the fragile pride of the dollar-earner in these matters.

'Sir, could you wait for a few minutes?'

A girl in a cotton sari, an outline of kohl around her eyes; he turned from her to gaze absently upon a rather innocent poster of a young, and apparently happy and affluent, couple filling in a form.

The girl continued to write for about five minutes. She was not aware that he was looking at her again; until he let his attention drift and shifted his gaze towards the other people in the bank.

'Sir?'

He had begun to daydream; it was him she was calling.

At last! She was looking straight at him. He shifted out of the sofa; he felt conscious of his largeness, but he used his imposingness unobtrusively on these occasions.

There was an air-conditioner behind her. (But this must be so much nicer than home, thought Jayojit, trying to imagine what her home must be like.)

'Sir, you wish to deposit fifteen hundred dollars into which account, savings or fixed?'

Her voice was girlish, but detached and polite; in spite of its lack of volume and insistence, it was clearly audible among other voices and transactions.

'Fixed,' he said after a moment. He was probably not as conversant with these terms as he should be.

He was transferring this money because, over the next two years at least, he'd be here for part of the year; that, after all, was the arrangement. Bonny was to be with him. Better to have some money earning interest when he was away. She bent her head to write something again. Jayojit luxuriated in the breeze coming from the air-conditioner. He noticed that there was no vermilion in the middle parting. The pleasure this artificial breeze gave him never lessened; it relaxed him whenever he happened to be in its path.

'I've never heard this name before,' she said, smiling. It was as if she'd let this slip out accidentally.

The absence of vermilion did not necessarily mean she was unmarried; at least, not these days any more.

'That's true,' he said, reluctantly drawn into the conversation. 'It *is* quite unusual.' He wondered again what 'Jayojit' exactly meant, and why his parents had given him this name. 'The one who is victorious over victory itself.' His parents must really have been straining to find a name that was new, a name not in common currency. And they had created this mutation. Then, as if in reaction, they'd given his younger brother quite a traditional name: Ranajit.

As if she'd noticed something or somebody, she said: 'Please give me a few minutes.'

Jayojit turned and saw a middle-aged man who'd probably been waiting behind him for some time return to a sofa where other customers sat. He absently held his passport in one hand, in case she needed it. A couple of minutes had passed and a girl from an enclave within called, 'Sunita, could you please complete this rupee draft, please?' Sunita, still attending to Jayojit, looked up and said, 'It's completed.' 'No, no,' said the other girl (she was dressed in a salwaar kameez), 'this one's to Bombay.' The woman did not reply for a few seconds; she was looking at the form; and then, plangently, 'Give me a few seconds, yaar,' she said. 'Ten different things ...' she muttered in a lower voice.

After some moments had passed, she continued in that low voice, murmuring her surprise to herself:

'Surajit I've heard of, and Ranajit—and I have a cousin called Biswajit ...'

At first he thought it was rain again, and then discovered it was the air-conditioner, its hum imitating the sound of a downpour.

Unlikely name for Ranajit, though, for a less war-like person one wouldn't find, nor one as absorbed in the small-scale promises of corporate work; or so Jayojit imagined.

None of this—*this* work—required special ability, he was sure; mainly dependability and some intelligence. She needed the money to buy her own saris and stick-on bindis. Maybe she had a boyfriend.

'My younger brother's called Ranajit,' he said.

She adjusted her sari, as if she knew she was being watched.

'What's the dollar like today?' he asked abrasively, as if asking after the health of a brash young relative who seldom fell ill.

She glanced behind her at a board, surreptitious, and murmured:

'Twenty-eight rupees today.' Then, looking down, she raised her face to him again.

'Sir, the interest rate's 14.5 per cent presently,' she said, smiling.

'I should put all my money in here,' he quipped loudly.

'The boy's still sniffling, isn't he?' said the Admiral. 'He shouldn't come to this city at all, it isn't good for him.' Mrs Chatterjee looked at her husband in disbelief, as if he'd uttered words which, like a prophecy, might come true; there is a saying in Bengali, 'Ku daak deko na', which warns against invoking unwanted things irresponsibly, in case the words have an effect and make them come into being.

After studying her grandson's symptoms, she thought it wasn't necessary to ask Dr Sen to make the trip downstairs; as he was a semi-retired doctor, there were times, paradoxically, when he was more difficult to get hold of than a practising one; and, anyway, he'd prescribe Incidal or Cosavil, whose names Mrs Chatterjee was familiar with. Looking after the Admiral had given her a compounder's familiarity with the names of the commoner drugs.

Yet the periodic sniffing cleared up in two days; whether because of Mrs Chatterjee's inspired diagnosis or because the microbe had lived its life they didn't know.

Meanwhile, Jayojit double-checked the date on his ticket; it was for the 6th of July.

'I suppose I should reconfirm it,' he said. 'In person.' What he meant was that he didn't trust Bangladesh Biman. He had a strong intuition that they wouldn't be available on the phone. Even in Claremont, getting through to the Detroit office had taken a resigned, mechanical tenacity and, simply, time; even a sort of stupidity. The phone would keep ringing, ringing.

'You know where the office is?' said his father, touching his beard.

'Yeah, I have a fair idea,' said Jayojit, with something like a shrug.

The date had been arrived at at random, but they needed to get back around then, when it was still summer. Their 'India trip' would have ended, a few of Bonny's friends, some of whom were new 'best friends' and lived near where he now lived with his mother and his mother's 'boyfriend', and some of the old ones he might look up in Claremont, would have been sent to summer camp by their parents. Some had gone on round-the-world trips with their families, parents or older brothers and sisters (Jayojit hazily recalled Bonny telling him that a girl he knew in class would be in Kathmandu with her older sister around the same time they'd be in India; they planned to go up the lower foothills of the Himalayas); it was difficult to say about the summer—it was a season when people went on holiday and you had no idea when exactly they'd be back. At any rate, Bonny would return to his mother in August 'Is it August or September?' the Admiral had asked Jayojit yesterday; 'No, August,' Jayojit had said—and he had no clear plans about what they'd do in Claremont till then.

'You could go back a week later,' said the Admiral; there was only the smallest hint of an appeal, implacable as a child's, in his voice.

'I keep forgetting how quickly it gets dark here,' said Jayojit, as if it were yet another peculiarity he'd discovered.

'Well, we're in the East,' said the Admiral, clearing his throat, speaking with the assurance of one who had been intimate with cartography. A light had been switched on in the sitting room.

Later, Jayojit went down to check if there was any mail in the letter-box. He did everything officiously, as if no task was unimportant; yet felt a mild apprehension when doing this self-imposed chore.

'Baba, wait for me!' said Bonny as he walked towards the door. 'Wait for me,' he repeated from inside.

'You want to come?' There was mild disbelief in his voice. For Bonny avoided the children downstairs. A wary look came to his face whenever their voices reached upstairs, and he'd go to his room and reread one of the three or four books he'd brought with him.

As they stepped out of the lift, lights were switched on. And by five o'clock in the morning there would be daylight again, earlier than almost anywhere else; his mother, after switching on the transistor radio that was tuned to Calcutta A, would water the plants, and then his father and she, after the first cup of tea to which both were addicted, and without which this early hour was sluggish, might go out for a walk. Then, returning, more tea, bowel movements, a rhythm to which they blindly adhered.

He crossed the hall, appearing larger than he really was, and walked towards the row of letter-boxes; bending, he opened his father's. The cries of children swelled behind him, and he almost expected to be collided with. There was nothing inside the narrow space, until he noticed a piece of paper folded vertically; an electricity bill; unblinking, his eyes went round it as he searched for the sum, one thousand five hundred and eighty rupees for the months of April and May (must be because the air-conditioner was running in his room these days); underneath it, he discovered there was an envelope. He bent forward and ran his finger clumsily through the top of the envelope, tearing it with short bursts of movement. Taking out a relatively small sheet of paper whose print could be seen faintly from its blank side, Jayojit read, with a look of amused disbelief:

Dear Madam,

We are pleased to say that Madamoiselle of Delhi is now in your area in Calcutta. Please visit us at between 9.30 a.m. and 6.30 p.m. on any day except Sunday and you will find a welcoming staff eager to cater to your interests. We have a wide range of salwaar kameez outfits, chunnis, Bolero jackets and we also stock decorations. Special discounts are available. Tailoring services are provided. Please lose no time in availing our services. We look forward to seeing you in the near future.

Yours sincerely,
Shaila Motwane

Some enterprising Sindhi woman. Shouldn't it be 'availing yourself of'? There was a chatty self-confidence in the tone that, in other circumstances, might have almost disarmed him.

He didn't see Bonny at first; for a second he mistook another boy for him, and then saw that he was leaning where a wall had thrown a shadow, against a pillar; a few children, some of whom Jayojit somehow seemed to know by sight, were playing around him—a Sikh boy; another curly-haired boy. As Jayojit advanced, Bonny waved to him. Jayojit waved back and shouted, 'Coming!' as the Sikh boy rushed past on roller-skates.

Near the steps was a group of teenagers in t-shirts. They were half-defined; in semi-darkness, as in the inside of a discotheque. They spoke softly to each other, not in Bengali, but in Hindi. 'This is their city,' thought Jayojit ruefully. 'Its future lies with them.'

'Want to play?' he said, leaning over his son and wiping his forehead.

'Not really, baba.'

Bonny'd never been shy at school or at home. He usually had two or three good buddies; Jayojit, from a past life, knew Ciaran, an Irish-American, and Ajay, a Gujarati doctor's son.

'Want to play with me, then?' asked Jayojit. 'What about it?'

He felt proud of the boy and, contradictorily, wanted to show him off while protecting him. Two boys were playing table-tennis on one side of the hall. They'd stop and one would announce 'Five two!' or 'Three love!', the louder to give the score a legitimacy, then resume the game at once.

'Hey, Ajit,' said a girl, eleven or twelve years old, stepping towards the table.

'Kya hai, bhai?' said the larger boy, his movements lazy after the last point.

'Give me the key, I'm going up,' she said. She blinked as the boy dug into his pocket.

'What happened to mummy?' asked the boy as he handed the key over, as if 'mummy' were a constant nuisance.

Play started again. There was a moment of hesitation after the game ended; then Jayojit went up to one of them and said, stammering courteously:

'I say … can we have a few shots … if you guys don't mind—just for a few minutes.'

'I don't mind, uncle,' the thinner boy said. 'It's okay, huh, Ajit?'

The boy, who'd voiced his exasperation about his mother not long ago, responded with an unequivocal gesture.

'Thanks, guys,' said Jayojit, looming over the two. 'Here, Bonny, see what you can do with this.'

They, Bonny's hair sticking to his forehead with sweat, played the simplest game, quite unlike the storm the other two had created; an uncomplicated give-and-take; Bonny's small frame had agility, but was still to acquire discipline. It wasn't a game, just an exchange of shots, measured and calculated. When either missed, they chased awkwardly after the ball and started again immediately. Everywhere the noise of children about their own breathless business surrounded them. After five minutes, Jayojit handed his racquet to one of the boys:

'I say, thanks, guys.'

'You're welcome, uncle.' The boys changed sides now.

'Let's take a small walk, and then we can go back,' said Jayojit.

There was a breeze; it seemed to have rained somewhere. A couple were in the compound, a lady in a chiffon sari and a man in white kurta and pyjamas beside her.

The moon, almost full, hung above this side of the building, staring at the balconies and clotheslines. No doubt this was significant in the almanac, a day of prayer in North India. His mother had told him only this morning, 'They'—meaning the women in a neighbouring Marwari family, a mother and her teenage daughter—'come to our flat to look at the moon from the bedroom window. Every year. Because it's not visible from their flat. They're very polite about it. The girl says, "Aunty, do you mind? It'll only take five minutes."'

'But why?' Jayojit had asked, incredulous, noticing his father loitering, introspective, by a cupboard.

'I don't know. There's something auspicious about it.'

Now the moon looked like a copper platter that a Marwari girl might have held in her hands. Climbing back up the steps to the hall, they found the boys gone and the table-tennis table free.

'Baba,' said Bonny, stopping before the table, 'we can play here now!' Visibly relieved that the others had gone.

'With what?' cried Jayojit. 'We can use our hands, but we'll have to dream up a ball.'

They walked towards the lift.

'Want to race me up the stairs?' asked Jayojit, turning. 'It's good exercise.'

But the lift had arrived; a woman emerged, holding a pomeranian by a leash. Bespectacled, she was about to pass Jayojit when she glanced at him and stopped.

'Mr Chattetjee, isn't it?' she asked sharply.

'Yes,' said Jayojit; he'd recognized her with an odd feeling of ambivalence. 'How are you, Mrs Gupta?'

'Quite well,' she replied, smiling as if she'd let slip a white lie. 'Not too bad. Back again from England?'

The pomeranian strained at the leash, and traced part of a circle; its paws made a glassy sound. Bonny gazed at the dog; he didn't like pomeranians, they were too perfect and toy-like.

'America, actually,' Jayojit said, apologetic; storing her words for future use in an anecdote.

'Oh! of course—(actually it's all the same to us here)!' she confided without embarrassment. 'But I much prefer the English accent, don't you? My God, I don't understand the American one at all!'

'No.' He added, 'It's strange to our ears,' speaking like one who hadn't been to that country himself, but also being truthful.

'And how long have you been here?' she asked brightly. 'A month and a half …' Time seemed to have passed more quickly in the last week than during the first half of the stay.

'One and a half months—in this weather! Really, what endurance you have, Mr Chatterjee! Go back to America, go back to America!' She broke into a piercing laugh that seemed to have nothing to do with what she'd just said. Then, solicitously, 'My niece in Cambridge is getting married,' she informed him.

The niece. Jayojit had never met her—he hardly knew Mrs Gupta—but ever since she'd heard that he taught economics, she'd told him that she had a niece at Cambridge—and last time, with her husband looking on, had said, 'But *you* have a Cambridge in Massachusetts, don't you?', as if briefly noting, and then choosing to give no importance to, a slightly compromising fact—and then felt obliged to provide him with auntly bulletins of her progress in England whenever she met him, which, as it happened, was two or three times a year; the niece, to his chagrin, had become a spirit who inhabited their conversations.

'That's very good! Congratulations!' Then, wondering why it should be the aunt who should be congratulated: 'When?'

'January,' she said.

'Cold time of the year—if it's in England.'

'Oh yes! I plan to go for the wedding.' The way she said this made it seem that the wedding was going to take place around the corner. 'I'll eat a lot and keep warm.' Then, as if she'd saved the most interesting nugget for the last, 'She's marrying an Englishman,' a little romantically. 'Anyway,' she sang, 'I must go now.' The leash in her hand became straight and taut. 'Mimi's urging me to go! I hope to see you again! Come on, Mimi,' she added in English, as if it were a language that came naturally with the pomeranian. She had altogether ignored his son, standing next to him.

When Jayojit had come to visit his parents a few years ago it was her husband, a man who'd been reduced by a stroke to shouting out his sentences, she'd been walking. A tall man in trousers and a bush shirt; part of the face had been paralysed, but it was the part that moved and spoke that looked disfigured. Although agitated, he took care to show that the agitation was directed at no one but himself, and, lifting his eyes, would manage to convey a smile. Mrs Gupta had gone about with him, her refusal to display any outward sign of discomfiture so marked that it was that that became noticeable. On the three days of Puja celebration, the man moved about with a light in his eyes, in a bush shirt he must have struggled to put on himself; and Mrs Gupta flitted between the sound of the drums and the children in new clothes. On Jayojit's last visit, soon after he'd arrived, alone, he'd learnt, in an aside during the first serious discussions they'd had about his divorce, that the gentleman had died; he'd had no time to register the fact; but when he'd seen Mrs Gupta again a few days later, she'd somehow seemed bereft without the hobbling man next to her.

'What a commotion!' said Dr Sen, shaking his head. Two men were repairing a pipe.

Jayojit said: 'I hope this doesn't mean that there won't be any water! We had a whole morning without water a few days ago.'

'Oh, no no,' the doctor said. 'I think this is a leakage. It's one of the things we discuss on Saturday.'

One of the men jumped back at a gush of water.

'Yes. The monthly meeting of the committee,' said Dr Sen. He said, like one reporting a scandal, 'The plumbing's old. It hasn't been looked into properly even once. They just ignore the problem, as if that'll make it go away.' Jayojit hadn't seen him so excited before; the doctor didn't explain who 'they' were.

Jayojit wasn't to know that Dr Sen was assertive before every meeting, but that during the meetings he kept quiet.

'But that's what he does!' protested the Admiral. 'I've seen him do it several times!' He looked glum but triumphant, like one who was to be vindicated yet again.

On Saturday, maidservants loitered downstairs; but by ten o'clock chairs had been arranged. Not that all the chairs would be needed, but they liked a sense of numbers, of largeness.

Dr Sen was among the early; he situated himself randomly, but near a fan. Heat was an unattributed participant in the debates; those nearer the fan's temperate zone were more reasonable. The people on the chairs increased, but no one seemed to know when or how the meeting would begin. Dr Sen acknowledged an acquaintance with a nod, and glanced once more at his watch.

Some of those attending had reappeared after a longish interval; a widower, Bhattacharya, spent half the year with one of his two daughters in Texas and had had open heart surgery; here he was, recently bathed, slightly darker, looking as if he'd never travelled beyond Sealdah or Kharagpur.

'When did you come back, Mr Bhattacharya?' said Dr Sen, with disproportionate friendliness, since they'd spoken not more than twice before.

'Day before yesterday.'

Just like that. The flat he'd left empty and locked must have needed clearing up.

There were others whom the doctor didn't recognize and who'd come to the meeting for the first time probably; they had the expectant, aimless air of people sitting on a park bench. Sengupta, who didn't get along with anyone, was by himself just as everyone else was, but he exuded this inability to belong.

'What time was it supposed to start, Mr Lahiri?'

Upstairs, the Admiral was inhaling as he combed his hair: 'I suppose I'll be late.'

'I don't see why you have to go,' said his wife; he looked at her, surprised.

'I have a responsibility too, you know, living in this building.'

After a moment he conceded: 'Sarkar's not bad. More educated than the rest, though he still looks like a menial ...' He paused aggressively after this, as if some ghost from the past might reprimand him. 'Then there's that fellow Ray, retired from Ahmedabad ...' he put down the comb, 'doesn't speak much though. But he's impressive-looking, always calm.' The Admiral was an admirer of the dignified mien. 'Subramanian's president this year. Not a bad sort. He talks too slowly.'

As he walked towards a door he said:

'Settled here for generations. Speaks Bengali like you and me.'

Mrs Chatterjee was only half-listening.

'Hasn't he ever greeted you during the Pujas? You won't be able to tell him apart from the rest.'

'I can't remember who he is. Maybe he *has* greeted me during the Pujas.'

Subramanian and Sarkar sat facing them. Whenever Subramanian began to speak the Admiral looked up.

About twenty people. There were factions; for instance, there was Sengupta, who'd brought disrepute upon himself and the committee during his presidentship last year. The Admiral looked at the back of his head, and the scattering of faces. He could see that Sengupta was feeling left out, that he was preparing for a confrontation, but wouldn't initiate it.

Dr Sen was daydreaming. The Admiral had a premonition

that he'd spend the meeting staring at the wall when, to his surprise, the doctor said: 'Why should we give contracts to two different parties for—uh, for maintenance of pipes and cleaning the waterworks? I don't understand.'

'Is that on the agenda for this meeting?' asked Sarkar, in the manner of one speaking of things pre-determined and transcending personal control.

'B-but it's a question of reducing costs'; sounding like the first, tentative notes on an instrument.

They spoke for the next twenty minutes of someone who, in spite of repeated reminders, failed to pay his 'outgoings' for the last three months. They referred to him, throughout, by his flat number. Now, reluctantly, they were planning to penalize 10C by cutting off his electricity supply; there was no choice in the matter.

A man in the third row was raising his arm; it was Sengupta; there was something tense about him, as if he were in the grip of a compulsion.

'Yes, Mr Sengupta?' said Subramanian, refusing to acknowledge a threat.

Without standing up, Sengupta said, 'Last year's budget has already been exceeded, Mr Subramanian.'

Subramanian moved his head to get a clearer view of Sengupta. Someone must have been in the first stages of catching a cold, or recovering from one, because he coughed repeatedly; Mrs Gupta looked distracted, as if life had turned out to be in some way a minor, uninteresting affair.

'We've gone into this before,' said Subramanian, not ready

to give up his control of the proceedings, but seeking to swerve delicately from a debate.

'That is not the answer I was looking for,' said Sengupta. This was evidently for the benefit of others. The Admiral was both bored and revived; he had stopped participating in these meetings, in rehearsing these platitudes about this fifteen-year-old building none of these people very much cared for; he knew that if he began to speak he would sputter and speak the truth. This was a different phase in his life, its significance, if it had any, not yet clear to himself; he no longer resisted the shape it took.

The matter was not resolved, and Sengupta's bull-like charge ended in nothing. In the next few moments the conversation actually drifted away from the question without anyone making it do so. The truth was that Sengupta could only make brief and histrionic stands but couldn't take up pursuit because he was vulnerable to questioning himself.

Half an hour later, the meeting was over.

'Is it more humid than last year?' the Admiral said to Dr Sen, standing in front of the fan.

But Dr Sen was taken with another matter.

'You see those postboxes. I th-think they're being vandalized. Two or three of them are broken—I d-don't know why: deliberately, or to steal mail.'

The row of deaf postboxes stared back at them.

'You never stay till September,' said Jayojit's mother, her smile private and ironical. 'You always go before.'

'God's sake, that's what the year's like,' said Jayojit; his mother seemed hurt, though she decided not to show it, at the outburst. He read her face; he was sorry. There was an anger in him, a frustration; whenever there was reason to be angry, he cut himself off. Instead, he reacted with impatience at some innocent remark, some item in the news; he'd come to a junction in his life where, over-alert, he was no more confident of being understood or of understanding others; but with his mother, especially during this visit, he had successfully held himself in check.

'You'll miss the Pujas,' she said. Last year they'd sat at home and listened to the drums beating downstairs and in the distance. They didn't visit anyone; instead, they spoke to Jayojit on the telephone.

'What are you doing, Joy?' his mother had asked. It was nine o' clock in the evening; a flurry of drums could be heard in the background, and the light that illuminated the balcony moved and had a tinge of colour to it.

'Nothing,' said Jayojit, sounding slightly at a loss. 'Of course, there's no holiday here, but I didn't have any lectures today. I've been at home.'

'Rana phoned today,' she said.

There was a small pause as those words travelled across continents.

'Really? What did he say?'

'He said they had guests and Anita made payesh.'

'Really, made payesh? Rana's a lucky fellow.'

When he was married, Amala and he'd go to Detroit (either

Detroit or Cleveland; but they preferred Detroit; they knew more people there) for the Pujas. Last time, the Detroit Puja Committee had hired two school buildings for the festival; and he'd bowed before the pratima with her large eyes, placed at one end of the hall near the portraits of the school founders. How fervent Amala used to be during the anjali! He used to wonder what she was praying for. She'd open her eyes after the anjali with a startled look, like a swimmer who's come up from underwater.

He didn't believe—belief did not come into it, as he'd explored the hall, cradling Bonny in one arm, or pausing clumsily to put him to sleep. (Half-asleep in that din, he'd grown heavier in his arms.) But, over the last few years, he'd begun to believe in the efficacy of prayer; of aloneness, which is what prayer was. That, to him, in the centre of the noise, had been a discovery.

'But this is what they do after it rains a little,' grumbled Jayojit's mother. She didn't explain who 'they' were. 'It's a good excuse.' Maya hadn't come.

'Where does she live?'

'Oh—not far away!' said Mrs Chatterjee, waving the question of distance away. 'Ghugudanga.' It sounded like a village; difficult to believe it was in the heart of Ballygunge. There'd been some waterlogging the past two days; that might have made things hard; but he was silent.

When he was a boy he'd come home from Ooty before the rains began. Some of his classmates were English, sons of diplomats, or of managers of companies still, in those days, sixty per cent British-owned; they took the changes in the weather cheerfully, 'Absolutely first-rate storm!', as they did their teachers, 'Chatterjee, I can never pronounce that man's name, yours is so much easier.' Come the rains, they'd vanish as if they'd muttered a mantra that made them dissolve into the atmosphere. The monsoons, like some messenger hurrying through the land, throwing his moth-like shadow, would have come to the South before he made his journey, so that he'd already have seen the large drops on his way to Bangalore, from where he set out for Delhi. Home was different places; Vishakapatnam, with the sea lashing the harbour, known by that quaint name at the time, Vizag; then Cochin; and Delhi, in Chanakyapuri, not far from Mrs Gandhi. 'Whatever you might think of her, she's gutsy,' the Admiral had said. 'The Russians respect her, the Americans fear her'; those words returning to him like the lines of a nursery rhyme. Even now, his father believed that India had declined since 'that woman's death'. Coming 'home', the habitation of the next four or five years in his adolescence, to these certainties; when his father was made Rear-Admiral, he recalled Nehru nostalgically, as if he were somehow responsible for all the good in people's lives: 'Met him, you know. Saluted him ... was it 'sixty-six? Broken man, but handsome. No truth to what they said about him and Edwina.' One would never have known that he was a commander at the time, and had been in Nehru's presence for only five minutes. Coming back from boarding school to a slightly altered set of parents, Joy'd still find some things unchanged, for instance his mother frequently reordering furniture in the bungalow, her movements as focused as a bird's, moving the Taj Mahals and shikaras. Outside one of the houses, there was a garden with oleanders in it; that was either in Vizag or in Delhi. A navy cadet stood outside the house all day. And Joy would lock himself up in his room, with the air-conditioner on, because it was sweltering in Cochin and the cleverest way of battling the heat was not moving. He read books he was too young for. Sometimes Ranajit, who was left to wander about the bungalow and was quite content to do so, would begin to bang on the door with primitive urgency to be let in—'Dada! Dada!'—the cry strangely plaintive.

Contact with the armed forces had cured them of the boyhood make-believe of wanting to be soldiers; instead, it was something else that took shape in them. Ranajit was less opinionated than Jayojit; and he'd had a love-marriage. Jayojit, after almost topping the list at Stephen's, had performed as expected at a scholarship interview, where he was questioned by, among others, Karan Singh, and had been surprised by his dark feminine eyes. The British Deputy High Commissioner, Pratt or Spratt, he couldn't recall, had asked him who his favourite authors were, and his mind had gone momentarily blank, his authors had deserted him, only one returned to him shadowly and he uttered his name: 'Pablo Neruda.'

'That's very interesting,' the Englishman had said, adding wryly, 'but wasn't he a diplomat? It seems we do some good things sometimes.'

There was a gentle murmur of laughter round the table, in

which Jayojit, just twenty-four years old, had joined nervously. Then the man had continued, 'Do tell us why, Mr Chatterjee.'

Jayojit always remembered his answer with a hearty laugh later: 'Had absolutely no idea what I was saying. Told him: "Because he's both political and sensuous. He reminds me of the Bengali poet Sukanta Bhattacharya." Can you believe such utter nonsense? I haven't even read Sukanta.'

But believe him they had, and it was he who'd turned down the opportunity to go to Oxford and accepted, instead, a rare scholarship to California: 'They have *seasons* there, baba!'

Karan Singh had, very mellifluously, asked him where he saw the future of Indian politics: 'Do you think we'll persist with the parliamentary system? Or adopt the presidential system?'

Jayojit half-listened; behind those kohl-dark eyes, he could only see the paradisial land of Kashmir. Not many years had passed since the Emergency; and, risking antagonizing the Congressman, he'd said: 'I think our parliamentary system needs to change, sir, but not towards the presidential system. If anything, it needs to be decentralized.'

Wasted words; in the end he'd found himself in America, where not everyone knew where India was. Yet that scholarship had taken some of his friends to England; one, 'Pugs' to his friends, had become an assistant editor of a national daily with the more sonorous name Rajen Mehra, and another a lecturer in Birmingham; yet another taught in the vast, wilderness-like campus of the Jawaharlal Nehru University—news came to him from unexpected sources, from hearsay, in which these fragments revealed a continuity. Meanwhile, Ranajit's 'romance' started when the family was in Delhi, when Jayojit had already left for the US. Ranajit was an undergraduate at the Hindu in 1982, would spend nights in secret at the hostel with his friends; and then his group of friends disintegrated and his mother decided he'd spend more time at home now, that he'd become 'serious' about his exams. But he'd go for walks in Lodhi Gardens—although Delhi was already reputedly unsafe after dusk—with a girl called Anita who was then only in Class XII in the Mater Dei School; or have milkshakes at Nirula's as blue-eyed tourists moved about in Connaught Place.

Jayojit could count the number of times he'd met his brother and sister-in-law after their wedding on the fingers of one hand. If anything was to blame, it was the ease of modern travel, which lulled people into believing that journeys to those closest to them could be postponed. His brother had called him 'dada'; Anita, the few times she'd seen him, called him 'Joyda'. They were to visit him at some point in the future in America. 'Come in September if you must,' he'd said brusquely to his sister-in-law. 'The Fall's really as lovely as it's supposed to be.'

It never rained like this where he lived. Not far away from Claremont, in Iowa, he'd heard there were thunderstorms; they were brought there by winds from the Gulf of Mexico. But where he lived, and where, till recently, Bonny and his mother had lived, there were contrary influences, for Claremont was washed by cool air from Canada. Once, when driving to college, he'd been caught in a hailstorm.

The college campus was off the motorway, four large buildings, two cafeterias, God knew how many lecture theatres, and a parking lot as huge as a desert. The college produced its own t-shirts, with 'Claremont' in Gothic letters inscribed upon them. When Amala had left him and gone to California, he used to wonder at how this town, with its McDonald's outlet guarding the highway at night like a lit oasis, had come to be so integrally a part of his life.

The doorbell rang at eleven, and it was Maya. 'Bus was late,' she said. Mrs Chatterjee said nothing.

Later, when Maya was in the kitchen and out of earshot, she whispered to her son:

'I shall be rid of her at the first opportunity.'

Maya, as if in belated response, let fall a utensil with a crash into the kitchen sink.

The next day: water had collected at the end of the lane that opened on to the main road. If you went down the corridor outside the Admiral's flat to the other end you might be able to espy some of the disorder that had been caused. Yet the post wasn't late.

'O ma,' he said, digging urgently in his trouser pocket, 'it's still here. I forgot to give you this.'

She peered—she had reading glasses, but rarely used them— at the leaflet advertising bolero coats and salwaar kameez sets.

'What'll I do with this?' Then, her mind moving on: 'Anyway, it might come in handy.' Was she thinking of a cousin's daughter,

Mahashweta, the only young woman in the family to whom they had, any more, a tangential relationship, for whom she might want to buy something if she came to Calcutta in the future?

'You might do some shopping there yourself.'

Jayojit's mother didn't have a sense of humour; or something handicapped its expression—because with her grandson she was almost nothing but teasing.

'For what, baba? Those shops are only meant for girls!'

When he'd married Amala, the salwaar kameez had just come into fashion; it had multiplied everywhere like a popular tune. Now, in its maturity, its prints were still multifarious and pleasing, like an annual blossoming.

Nothing in the post today except a statement of interest for the Admiral. Three months after their wedding Amala had begun to write to her mother-in-law from Arlington. The letters came with Mrs Chatterjee's name on the envelope, Mrs Sumitra Chatterjee, in a neat running hand at first unfamiliar. They were determinedly chatty but formal, and full of questions, perhaps to camouflage some sense of inadequacy, about how things were at 'home'; and, slow but destination-bound, they took two or three weeks to get here. To Mrs Chatterjee they had given a fleeting pleasure, and also the obligation of having to reply in simple, serious sentences that were, however, laboriously composed; for she was a poor letter-writer.

What had made him marry her? Was it her prettiness, which he'd been struck by the first time he'd seen her in their new house in

Jodhpur Park? 'Hi, I'm Amala.' Every word pronounced carefully, her lips becoming a small 'o' at the middle syllable of her name. Then transformed, in Thyagaraja Hall, into a graven image, small and adorned, head shrouded by the sari. There had been some confusion about the details; West Bengalis carried the bride around the fire; in East Bengal—and he'd thought this was true of Bengal in general—she walked round it. Moreover, before the meeting of the eyes, the 'shubho drishti', in West Bengal, a large betel leaf was held in front of the bride's face; this was news to him. And her face, lit intermittently by the camera's flash—not very Bengali, almost North or North West Indian, no hint or tracery of high cheekbones, but, in her forehead and mouth, a suggestion of elsewhere (she'd told him that her ancestors were brahmins who'd moved to Bengal from Sind several generations ago, seeking sanctuary).

On their way to the States, she changed from a Patola to a pair of jeans in the airport—'Can you believe it, it's the first time I'm going abroad?'; sitting late into the night, they'd talked about their families. In the eighties, travelling to the West or to America was still uncommon—after arriving, they'd been in Arlington for a few months before moving to Claremont, and she'd found the desert climate hard going: 'Baap re, it's hotter here than Cal!' 'Cal' was Loreto House, the Sky Room, Middleton Row, New Market, Loudon Street, Tollygunge. In Claremont, he'd told her they were now only three hours away from Canada, and that year had been a year of expeditions; the Niagara Falls, roaring behind them as they posed for a photo, the underground shopping malls in Toronto. 'Don't you want to continue studying Pol Science?'—sometimes, for fun, he'd imitate some of her habits of speaking—and she'd made a face and said, 'I want to be a housewife.'

She began by phoning her parents twice a week, speaking loudly over the mouthpiece as if she were talking to people in the next room (most of the conversations took place in his absence, or at odd times of the night in the living room; later, he'd imagine their content when stopping at the time and duration printed on the telephone bill; it was her mother, he knew, who was her confidante, and could chatter and whisper with her daughter as if she were her twin sister, while with her father Amala, on the phone, was still the flirtatious, slightly high-pitched, little girl, always being reprimanded for not realizing it was a long-distance call); nevertheless she was, and this was hardly noticeable at first, distancing herself from 'Cal'. The satisfactions of life had made her clear-sighted: 'Jayojit, you're too cynical. Baba, you know you're here for the money and the good life like the rest of us! What's wrong with that?'

He went out in the afternoon, to buy a bottle of antacid to counter the dyspepsia his long spells of inactivity had brought on, and one of Nescafé instant coffee (which, contradictorily, increased the dyspepsia)—they'd run out of coffee this morning. He'd done everything on this trip to avoid meeting people he knew and to occupy himself in small ways so that he might forget the trip was coming to an end. Walking down had hardly an effect on him;

he breathed soundlessly. On the second floor he was delayed by the sound of discordant music; taking a few steps into the corridor and craning his neck, he saw through an open doorway a gathering of Marwari women and children singing bhajans, the children on laps and a large woman beating out the rhythm on a pair of cymbals; he turned, and resumed his journey downward. At the end of the last flight (now he could see the lift descending on the ground floor from the landing, the doors parting by themselves and revealing the liftman half-asleep inside) his way was blocked by two women, maidservants, deep in conversation so that they didn't notice him.

He went into the hall and compound and then towards the main road, thinking about the days left. This time he went past the Birla temple, with its fake North Indian architecture, and then walked on towards Gariahat. He walked past Mizoram House, and moved towards the area he'd visited repeatedly; the Grindlays Bank, Rash Behari Avenue, the bookshop he'd gone into once. At the crossing of Gariahat and Rash Behari Avenue, he, unable to hear himself think in the noise, bought a chequered duster from the pavement for twelve rupees. Then, from a chemist's and provisions shop, he bought the antacid and the coffee, which, to his incredulity, cost fifty rupees, and, to compensate, came with a free frisbee of rudimentary appearance.

On his way back, he slowed down, and stared at a building in the early stages of construction; clusters of rods coming out of the earth. Where was it he'd seen it before?—from the other end of the fourth-floor balcony. Now trees and windows concealed it; but was it already in a more advanced state of construction than he'd seen it in, or was it his imagination? Barely conscious of them, he passed the old-world (by old-world he meant the fifties and the sixties, where everything seemed more sacrosanct than at any other point in India's history, except perhaps its Golden Age) bungalows of the rich Marwari entrepreneurs, with their large gates; and then some more recent six- or seven-storeyed buildings with balconies. He'd realized recently (it had been inarticulate in him since God knows when, but he understood it only now) that, given a choice of being born at any time in India's past, he'd have chosen to be born in the thirties, so that he could have a taste of the first years of post-Independence India: and he entertained this fancy almost as if it might be a possibility. Instead, he'd been born just after the mid-fifties. Now, unconnected to this, like the smell of dust, a snatch of a conversation returned; idly, he turned over again in his head the idea of a second marriage, which the Admiral had been proposing to him last evening.

'It's not as bad an idea as you think.' A silence as on cue.

'I don't think it's a *bad* idea. But—once bitten twice shy, as they say.'

He didn't mean his first, and only, marriage. He meant the meetings he'd had with Arundhati seven months ago. One meeting, then two, then three; more cups of tea. She respected him in her quiet way—he'd felt that; and he'd begun to like her. In spite of an 'arranged marriage' having failed once, they were both prepared to give it a second go; he still didn't have confidence in 'love'; it was other things—understanding, mutual needs—that held a marriage together. 'But not a Hindu wedding, God, no; I couldn't take another one of those,' she'd said. 'Just a registry.' Everything had been going smoothly and then, almost without warning, he'd realized, after a little more than a month, that something was holding her back, she'd changed her mind and wouldn't go through with it.

His father, scowling in his beard, was more resilient than he was. The Admiral had already had a vision of the second wedding.

'By the way,' Jayojit asked—and he'd never put this question before; months had passed—'what happened to her?'

The Admiral had to furrow his eyebrows before he could understand what he was talking about. Once he'd understood, he waved one hand. In his other hand he held a tumbler in which he'd poured a peg of the Chivas Regal ('These damn monsoon breezes can make you feverish') that Jayojit had brought.

'Don't know.' Almost childish; and certainly prickly.

'No. I see,' Jayojit said.

Their conversations came back to him, like snatches drifting to him from a neighbouring window.

A watchman was guarding the still-skeletal structure. 'How long?' he said to the watchman in Hindi. The watchman looked startled. 'Kitna din lagega khatam hone ko?' As if he was planning to buy a flat here. 'Saal lag jayega, saab,' the watchman. A whole year for completion!—had the contractor adopted some sort of go-slow policy? Property prices still weren't as high as in Bombay: but they were high enough. He couldn't make sense of it; maybe it was deliberate—so that prices might appreciate *while* the building was in construction. 'Kya naam hoga?' he asked, making a perfect arc on the dust with one shoe. Lines appeared on the watchman's forehead as he tried to think. Then the lines vanished; a smile parted the lips. 'Manjusree Apartments, saab.' Ugly, old-fashioned name, thought Jayojit, but what you'd expect from a nouveau-riche building. They talked about the building delicately, as if it could hear them. He walked back towards the temple; everywhere there were creepers, with white blossoms, and gulmohur trees; he thought of some of the lanes in Delhi, genteel Greater Kailash. Had he been here last time?—he couldn't remember things clearly from last time, confusion dominated, talk about courts. From the building coming up crows took off, probably disturbed by something; they might have built a nest there.

When it began to rain, he took refuge at the entrance to the auditorium by the Birla temple, beneath the images of elephants and gods. It was still bright; rain and sun at once, like an electric floodlight playing upon the water. Then, when it stopped, the moisture seemed to ascend as steam off the road.

Coming into his lane, he saw someone ahead of him. It was Mrs Gupta; he realized about two weeks had passed since he'd last seen her. He wondered about her life after her husband's death; for he presumed—vaguely remembered—that she had no children.

He was walking faster than her, so that, by the time they had entered the gates, he was just a little behind her. She must have felt his presence, because she glanced back at him swiftly.

'Ah—Mr Chatterjee!'

They walked together the rest of the way. She told him how she'd had to take shelter beneath a tree, standing next to a man vending Hindi paperback novels, from the shower. And yet, this time, Jayojit felt, the monsoons had never arrived properly.

'No umbrella!' she said, opening the palm—small and startlingly fair—of one empty hand. 'How could I know? No clouds, nothing!'

'Out visiting someone?' he asked politely as they came up the steps. He said this in Bengali. 'Kaarur baadi giye-chhilen?' He stared at a small black dot on her forehead, which seemed to avert his gaze. Her eyes moved from one side to another, like an animal's that has been genuinely surprised by a shower.

'Oh no,' she said. She had a plastic packet in one hand, and was wearing a printed sari, pretty but now faded. 'No, I just went to a shop and bought a few things.'

'Luckily, this place is close to two markets,' she said in explanation. 'My daughter, who lives in Alipore—the old "white town"—says there are no markets nearby, it's a great problem sending out a servant to do the shopping.' That put paid to his notion about her being childless. Her eyes, to him, still expected much of life, but everything else about her seemed to inhabit a world of routine and slightly aimless repetition. She lifted the packet and he could see, through the plastic, a bottle of disinfectant liquid. 'This is quite good!' she volunteered. 'Mr Chatterjee, we're getting some of your conveniences here too!' In reply, he showed her the frisbee, and she stared at it very seriously. 'Free gift,' he said. They waited together for the lift. The numbers on the little panel above the door to the lift decreased from six downward, and they seemed to be standing for a disproportionately long time. She seemed to be less forthcoming now than she'd been the other evening; probably had something on her mind. At any rate, although she must know something about his own life—his story being fairly well known—she had the kindness not to mention it; or was probably not interested; had her own life to think about. When the doors of the lift opened, he heard the loud hum of the fan inside, and said:

'After you.'

'Baba,' said Jayojit, counting the foils of the traveller's cheques, 'I may as well change these.' The Admiral looked up from the paper and considered them with suspicion, as if they were counterfeit money. Yet Jayojit didn't want to have to go again; he calculated his remaining expenditure to be about 2,000 rupees, including the parting bakshish to Maya—his mother and he had discussed this; she, with characteristic prudence, had said seventy-five rupees; he'd decided, after some thought, on the more appropriate sum of a hundred and fifty—and the airport tax: in his head he computed the figure of roughly seventy dollars. (His mother was on the verandah, looking out at two part-time helps coming in.) Only the day before yesterday he'd been to Grindlay's again to put money into his account and withdraw a further five thousand; this was the five thousand he gave each month to his parents, after protests on their side and laborious dismissals on his, to cover expenses. (It was true that he anyway dominated his parents; whether consciously or not, he couldn't tell; but he often felt, for no justifiable or clear reason, he knew better. In fact, soon after he came back, this was the role he was asked, not in so many words, to assume.) There was another girl, fair and rather small, at the desk this time, with a conspicuous, large stick-on bindi on her forehead, not Sunita, the dark one, talkative and industrious by turns, who'd been there last time.

He'd needed trivial information: his balance of account. He'd felt lost; glanced in confusion and with something like contempt at the customers sitting meekly on the sofa; then this girl, at the table nearest him, had come to his rescue with a 'Yes, sir, can I help you, please?' which he hadn't heard the first time; like a line in a child's poem, she'd had to repeat it. She'd given him a print-out, bending her head and ignoring the noise the printer made.

Today's rate in the *Statesman*, in a row of crowded figures, was Rs. 29.00 to a dollar. Like mercury in an imaginary thermometer, this number rose and fell and rose. He turned back to the first page to double-check the date and that it was indeed the day's newspaper; then he returned to the page at the back to scan, painfully, once more for the figure he'd noted not long ago.

Jayojit left Bonny at home with his grandparents. 'This is not a fun trip,' he said.

He was wearing a light pink twill shirt that had, somehow, been left untouched during this trip.

It had rained in the morning, a dark drama of distant noises that had spent itself after the dawn; wheels had slashed through the wet road and left marks that had still not dried. He did not have to search for a taxi; there was one on the main road; the driver, he noticed, had only one good eye, and was wearing thick spectacles behind which his eyes swam liquidly. 'Old Court House Street,' Jayojit said, leaning back heavily. The driver nodded; he had a learned, superannuated look about him.

Old Court House Street he associated not with the American Express Bank, but with the Great Eastern Hotel, to which he'd been as a child of ten; they'd gone on someone's birthday, probably his mother's. At the time it wasn't the celebrated catacomb it was now, but still a hotel where people stayed; but Jayojit's picture of it came from word of mouth and family anecdote, because he actually had no memory of it or of the famous Chinese restaurant they were supposed to have gone to. In fact, he wasn't even sure where his father was posted at the time and what they were doing in Calcutta.

'Take it through Lower Circular Road,' said Jayojit. Morning traffic faced them everywhere; to offer a route from a limited number of alternatives was not to be any more ensured of a quicker journey than to turn a few names in your head and mutter one hopefully.

They passed the Chief Justice's bungalow, an island flanked by potted plants. Absent-mindedly, he felt the rim of the brown paper envelope he was holding in one hand and which he'd lifted from a pile of the Admiral's correspondence; he'd put his passport and the traveller's cheques inside it (must be careful not to lose it), he two kilograms lighter and a few shades unreally darker in the passport photograph taken in a booth in Claremont's small downtown drug store three years ago, when the old passport in a drawer had suddenly expired and given up its ghost, and he had been at a loss about how to apply for a new one, and had daydreamed, or day-nightmared, of forms and registered-post slips.

They were stuck behind a bus; with every vibration, it sent a burst of exhaust fumes into the taxi. The driver seemed unperturbed; embracing the steering wheel with both hands, he seemed to be staring at the advertisement for a cooking oil on the back of the bus. He inhaled the air which absorbed the exhaust as soon as it had threatened to darken it.

Above the buildings, one behind the other, Eveready battery, Sonodyne television videos, etched against a netlike background which would begin to glow at twilight. Obediently, as if he'd been commanded to, he read the messages. There was a large Asian Paints sign, already heralding the Pujas, which this year would begin in late September. Two large eyes, presumably Durga's, filled the hoarding, and the message, Celebrate With Asian Paints.

'Traffic today,' said the driver.

There was a pause. At the driver's ironic observation, the other noises receded accommodatingly, and the driver's voice somehow grew louder than the orchestral background of engines.

'Yes,' Jayojit said, lamely. He never knew what to do when someone spoke to him uninvited. His self-confidence actually hindered him when he was asked to interact with a person well outside his social sphere. Then, against his better judgement, although he knew the question was as rhetorical as the driver's gambit, added, 'Always like this in the morning?'

'Much more,' said the driver in broken Bengali. 'Let a drop of rain fall and you will see what happens.' For good measure, he appended the generalization, neither turning back nor looking at the rear-view mirror, 'Chowringhee not good road.'

Passing the Chief Justice's bungalow had reminded Jayojit of Amala's father; it was both surprising and fortunate that they hadn't run into each other since the divorce. They'd had many common friends, moved in the same circles ... Indeed, both his father and Amala's were on first-name terms with the Chief Justice. By the time of the marriage, Jayojit had a good relationship going with Mr Chakroborty; so that, at the time of the ceremony (Mr Chakroborty bare-chested and dhuti-clad), they'd exchanged a smile at the start and the man had shrugged his shoulders, as if they were two proud brahmins enacting but tolerantly disowning the rigmarole of Hindu ceremony. Jayojit had attended the wedding something like a tourist; he was one of those who had no time for tradition, but liked, even in a sentimental way, colour and noise; so he'd reacted to the smoke and fuss of ritual with the irritation of a visitor in a traffic-jam, but had said, with genuine delight, 'Absolutely wonderful: Bismillah Khan!' when he'd heard the sound of the shehnai. Last time Jayojit had heard—he couldn't remember from whom— that Amala's father had become a lawyer at the Supreme Court and was posted at Delhi. Amala's father was quite a bit younger than Jayojit's—probably twelve or thirteen years—a man whose family had settled in these parts for generations. Amala's father had eventually moved out of the ancestral house in Tollygunge; Jayojit had been more than once to the two-storeyed house in

Jodhpur Park the man had constructed for his own family, the ground floor divided into a sitting room and a study; on the first floor were the bedrooms, bookshelves, and dining room.

But this time, Jayojit hadn't been in that area even once. He could never, anyway, distinguish one lane from another in Jodhpur Park, nor make any sense of the way the houses were hurriedly, almost frantically, numbered, as if the planner, when conceiving of this serene and perfectly pleasant area, had had a train to catch.

A horn blew near his ear. 'Saala!' whispered the driver, and wrenched the gear; it's these elderly ones that are the most violent, thought Jayojit in surprise. The envelope rested in his left hand; he moved it to his lap.

Outside the Express building, he parted with a rupee coin to a boy of twelve or thirteen. On the first floor, it was cool, as if he'd climbed the stairs to mountainous Tibet, or found himself near Shangri-La. But he had a faint premonition and a memory of the country he'd come from not long ago. There wasn't much of a queue; three people, who had the air of harmless scavenging birds about them, and must therefore be travel agents, and the back of a European's head, fine, pale gold. A bearded Bengali sitting on the sofa with his daughter. Something about the colour of her skin, milky-pale, next to her father's light brown, suggested her mother was European. He turned from them. Jayojit looked about until his eyes found what they were seeking; the buying rate on the board: Rs 29.30 to the dollar—thirty paise more than what the *Statesman,* in its more conservative speculation, had promised.

'He doesn't like fish,' said Mrs Chatterjee. She had a martyred look.

'Well, I've had my fill of fish,' said Jayojit, patting his stomach.

'You don't feel *hungry* when it's *hot*,' said Bonny, struggling to emphasize every important word.

The Admiral's hair was lifted by the breeze. 'It's a lovely time of the year,' he said.

'Lovely time or no lovely time,' his wife said, 'it gives me a headache with that woman not coming these days and the clothes drying so late.'

The Admiral got up from his armchair and stretched himself. 'Haven't been out walking for a couple of days now,' he said. 'But it's risky these days in the morning.'

Last night he hadn't slept well; it had been humid; he'd grunted as he'd turned from side to side, snored and then woken up; and, unknown to his wife, had, in the dark room, gone over the next months, envisioning the various scenarios. It was only when thinking of his grandson that he calmed down into acceptance; got up and grunted, 'Ektu aram hoyechhe,' acknowledging, in a low tone, that the heat had ebbed. Mrs Chatterjee was asleep; they had this habit, both of them, of addressing each other even when the other was out of earshot. Then, groping but familiar with the lefts and rights of the path, he'd gone into the kitchen to drink some cold water.

'I'd like to go somewhere during the monsoons. To a dryer place. It's not that I don't like the monsoons. It's just that there's too much water in South Calcutta.' But he couldn't remember when he'd last had a holiday and he had no plans of having one. In his present state of mind, he didn't particularly like being at home, but if there was one thing he liked less, it was going somewhere else.

'Strange thing for a seaman to say,' said Jayojit, a leg extended on the table.

'Oh, ships are extremely dry places. They have to be.' He paused, and said, 'Suffered a lot from seasickness myself.'

'I suppose you could go and stay with Ranajit.'

With Ranajit, who'd grown up with his parents, moving wherever they did ('I can't have *two* boys living away from me,' Mrs Chatterjee had, distraught, insisted), the relationship between father and son had probably been closer but subject to more strain; Ranajit making the sacrifice of changing schools, of sets of friends whose oddities were no sooner memorized than they were replaced by another class, another school anthem.

'Oh no,' said the Admiral, waving one hand repeatedly. The room with its old painting (bought from a gallery from an artist they knew slightly; 'Charity begins at home,' the Admiral had joked) and decorations was lit by the lightning outside the verandah. The Admiral said, 'I don't like going back to places where I've worked.'

Jayojit had to reconfirm the Bangladesh Biman tickets.

On the way to Chowringhee the roads were strangely empty; he wondered if it was a holiday and then thought, 'Of course it isn't.' Ashutosh Mukherji Road and Bhowanipore were deserted, as on the day of a strike, and he decided it must be the time of the day. As the taxi passed the Aeroflot office, with its huge blue and white sign, he thought, with a sigh, of the stories he'd heard about it, which made him self-congratulatory even about having a Biman ticket. 'Given a choice between a Muscovite and a Bangladeshi,' he thought as the taxi halted at a crossing, 'I'd plump for the latter.' He shook with laughter when he remembered how a friend, on his way to Cambridge, England, had been humiliated when changing planes in 1986, and spent an endless night in an unheated Moscow airport. Then, as the taxi moved forward again, the smile was replaced by a look of exasperation when Jayojit recalled one of his father's cousins, Pramathesh jethu, who used to swear by Aeroflot—'It's good, solid food they serve you, I tell you; who wants fancy trappings?'—most probably because he was a member of the Communist Party of India in his youth, and had

160

actually travelled three or four times in his seventy-two-year-old life to Russia; until he contrived to die, diplomatically, one year before the break-up of the Soviet Union.

The Biman office was crowded; the queues disintegrated in a mixture of high spirits and panic. Jayojit stood facing a poster with an elegant woman sitting by a fountain. This would be Rome or Vienna. The glass door opened whenever someone came in and the pavement outside became visible, and the noise of the traffic on Chowringhee amplified until the door closed again.

'Right!' he said when he'd got back. 'I've performed the Himalayan task. The worst is over.'

It had actually made him mad with rage; there'd been a man ('If one can call him that,' thought Jayojit) behind him in the queue who'd taken a liking to him and kept prodding him in the back to ask in dialect: 'Brother, which is the line for refund?' But Jayojit had a way of not showing his emotions. Now he'd brought with him the two tickets with the new tags stuck to the counterfoil. Attached was also a ragged computer printout infested with tiny numbers; the nocturnal, ever-unfamiliar language spoken at airports; 2300 for eleven o'clock; 0000 when midnight was meant.

'What time does it leave?' asked the Admiral, petulant at his own ignorance.

'Seven-thirty,' said Jayojit. 'And then it reaches Dhaka at eight, I think. I can't remember if they're behind us or ahead of us. Anyway, it's only a half an hour difference. The plane for New York, fingers crossed, leaves at eleven.' He paused after this cheerful recital, and then said, 'They didn't ask me whether I wanted vegetarian or non-vegetarian. Maybe I was expecting too much!'

'I hear they give ilish sometimes,' said his mother. 'At least that is what I hear.' As if she were speaking of a wedding where it was rumoured a certain dish was bound to be served.

'Ilish in mustard,' said Jayojit with mock distaste. 'We can eat it with our fingers!'

Coming out of the office he'd walked down Chowringhee, one with a stream of people indistinguishable from office-goers. He passed the Lighthouse Cinema and the Grand hotel; no perceptible breeze; not long ago he'd been amidst the traffic on the left and now he was hardly aware of it. He had wanted to buy a few things before he left—to give away as presents to some of those he knew in Claremont. And a few things for his own home.

'Cottage Industries?' he said. 'They have one here, don't they?'

'Yes,' said the Admiral, standing in the middle of the room and thinking, as if the city were whirling around him. 'Haven't been there for a long time.'

'It's near the Metro Cinema,' said Jayojit's mother.

'All those lovely Rajasthani bedcovers,' said Jayojit, 'and pichwais and tables—they cost a fortune in America.' He'd laughed rather loudly and said to his father: 'You have to hand it to these Rajasthanis, with those traditions going way, way back! In the end, what do we Bengalis have except a few first-class university degrees—and a good command of English?'

He came back with two mirrorwork cushion covers, a bedcover for himself, and two small brass birds for his neighbour, a cardiac surgeon. 'You can buy endlessly from that place, and you have to hold yourself back,' he chuckled. There was a pichwai, in particular, he'd stood before silently, undecided whether to buy—it had reminded him of one that hung in his drawing room when he was married, and this was what, in the end, went against it with a Krishna at the centre, surrounded by ten or twenty Krishnas and Radhas dallying with each other, their mystic union replicated like raindrops. He'd suddenly become aware that his mind had been caught in the rippling dance of the picture. 'No time to waste,' he'd admonished himself.

He'd also bought a sari for his mother. It was a pretty sari, an off-white tangail with orange embroidery upon it, and a green border. 'Joy, it must have cost a lot,' she said. He had lighted upon this tangail not because it had stood out but because it had held back; there had been an understated quality about it that had caught his attention. 'Consider it a Puja present,' said Jayojit.

She was really more interested in the other things, however, turning them over, scrutinizing them with a firm gaze, trying to make the imaginative leap, to see them through the eyes of the people Jayojit would give them to. From this arose an unarticulated thought within her, concerning what kind of friends he had, and what beauty they found in these Indian handicrafts. 'Look at these, ma, they're lovely,' said Jayojit, unfolding the cushion covers. A taste for regional handicrafts had developed in him since he'd begun to live abroad, and one day he'd begun to look at one table cloth, one cushion cover and another with new eyes, comparing, evaluating. His mother liked the bedspread in her quiet way, and was attempting to picture, in her mind's eye, what it would look like in her son's bedroom. 'It'll look very bright over *there*,' she said at last. Jayojit refolded the cushion covers.

Bonny had picked up one of the brass birds, and was trying to make it fly.

'Put it back, Bonny,' said his father. 'It's not a toy.' Then he said to his mother, 'This Cottage Industries is big, all right, but the Delhi one's much bigger, isn't it?'

'Oh, what are you saying, Joy,' a shadow passed over her face and she smiled reminiscently, 'it's about three times this one's size.'

He remembered he'd overslept on one of those days last year when he'd had an appointment with his lawyer in the morning. It was a late summer's day; dahlias in bloom, hawthorn, roses on the hedges. His neighbour was in the garden; he'd retired now, but was still a consultant to a few hospitals, and he lectured as well, and gave to charities; once or twice Jayojit had been startled to see a horse in the garden, and the doctor's six-year-old granddaughter sitting upon it. As he came out on to the doorstep, the cheerful cardiologist said:

'Hi, Jay. Everything OK?' The suburb they were in was on an elevation, and a road dipped and descended towards the town. ('The second poshest area in Claremont,' Bonny'd surprised Jayojit by saying a month before his mother left with him; strange what children will pick up from adult talk.) From strategic vantage-points the little map of Claremont could be seen below, including Gary the lawyer's five-storey office: Bernstein, Paretski and Smith; and then the surrounding country unfolding.

Jayojit had smiled and said:

'Everything's fine, Leo.'

Leo's life had arrived at some kind of a plateau, a flatness where there was only horizon, at least that's what it looked like from the outside. Three marriages; numberless children and children's children—thousands, millions of hearts repaired, and his own red with haemoglobin. Jayojit's own lot, despite his assurance to Leo, had been like one of the quinine pills he'd had to swallow hastily during this visit to Calcutta. He liked talking to this large, red man; none of the chitter-chatter he heard in the universities; feminism, which he considered an intellectual plague (how many arguments he'd had when he'd voiced his views!); careers and conferences. Late in the afternoon, Jayojit got up to begin arranging things for the departure, including the brass birds he'd bought for his neighbour. He opened the cupboard doors, peering inside, taking out a few of his shirts, closing them again, his mind, like an insomniac's in the repose of the afternoon, returning to odd bits of conversation, including a ridiculous discussion he'd found himself having with a Jewish colleague, one of those men who called themselves 'feminist', in which he'd argued vociferously that America had taken away the constraints of the institution of marriage but replaced them with nothing else. 'We can't live without constraints,' he'd said. 'Even the—no, *especially* the free-market economy is held together by tiny rules more subtly graded than the caste system!'

Then, going into the kitchen, he poured himself a glass of water from a bottle that had been left in the pantry. It had a flat taste; it was water in appearance and name only—he opened the fridge and shook out a few cubes from the ice tray into the glass. He drank impatiently, as he did everything, as if he were using up the moment.

In the half-open fridge, into which he once more put the ice tray, shone the small light; he closed the door; when he was a boy, returning home for the summer, he'd wonder, as if it were a matter far more important than his studies, whether the light stayed on even after the door was closed, and, if so, what the fridge's sealed but lit world was like in the inside. It was an old fridge—he coughed solitarily and supposed he could buy his parents a new one; maybe on his next visit, when things had settled down a little. The smells from today's lunch's leftovers had escaped the fridge, came faintly to him, reminding him of what he'd eaten not more than two hours ago. He'd seen the food, daal with a shadow fallen over it, the patient head of a pabdaa fish, its eye chilled in its socket, placed on the racks in small stainless steel bowls.

Stepping out, he saw his mother asleep, her face in the pillow, her arm around Bonny. The sight, for no particular reason, made him smile, as if he'd accidentally beheld an odd and funny sight. He himself, surgically halving his growing up, as if it were a living thing which could somehow be distributed democratically, between Ooty and wherever his parents happened to be, hadn't had much chance to experience closeness.

Going out into the hall, he noticed something glinting on the table. Bending, he saw it was part of the counterfoil for one of his father's medicines—this one was for high blood pressure, Enapril; he'd heard the name on his mother's tongue; she pronounced it 'Annapril', abstractedly and in passing, as if it were some Christian woman's name. He picked it up and threw it into the dustbin.

Jayojit's father was snoring. It wasn't a comfortable sound; it was an irregular wheezing, as if the Admiral had carried over some complaint to the world of his sleep. Near the verandah, Jayojit became conscious, for the first time, that the wall of heat had gone; it was still hot, no doubt, but the powerful heat which attended the verandah was absent. He saw now that it was actually raining, a spray like drizzle that whirled in the air before it fell.

Before the sun went down, Jayojit and Bonny were standing in the verandah when Jayojit saw a kite through the grille. It had perched on a dripping pipe, its brown feathers catching the remaining sunlight; the sun journeyed behind it, towards the cricket fields of the club. 'It's an eagle, an eagle! I saw it another day, too!'

'That's a kite,' said Jayojit, glancing down at his son's head.

'It's an eagle,' said Bonny. 'I've seen them in San Diego.'

'It's a kite,' said Jayojit again. 'Not the kind of kites people fly. It's a bird called a kite.'

'What are you two talking about?' asked Jayojit's mother, standing in the hall. 'I could hear your voices.'

He'd gone downstairs, and he ran into Dr Sen.

'Out for a walk?' he said, ambling towards him.

The doctor's complexion looked a shade darker than usual. He ran a hand over his forehead, disturbed, in an uncharacteristic, nervous gesture, a few tracings of hair on his bald head.

'For a walk … heh—no, not at this time of the day,' he said, shaking his head and smiling. 'Besides, you know, one can't walk about in Calcutta these days. There are one or two places,' he waved around himself, as if delineating his set of choices, 'not many.' He looked at Jayojit, smiled, beholding him with the eyes of one who, in the midst of change, can only offer a sort of continuity, and said, 'No, I had come to see if I had any letters.' And he did have a few letters in his hand.

'Expecting anything?'

'Not really,' said Dr Sen, deprecatingly. As if admitting to an embarrassing, simplistic fact: 'Well, a nephew of mine sends me the *Smithsonian*. It's a very good magazine—you must know it. The pictures, the *details!* Even the *paper's* very good.' He shook his head, 'The last issue had a *t-tremendous* chapter on ancient Egypt; lovely pictures of the mummies and the pyramids; *strange* things, pyramids, when you think about them; I hear they used to put the pharaohs' cats inside with the pharaohs—I don't know how they found out about these things!'; the old Bengali romance for arcane, often useless bits of knowledge transformed his expression briefly. Then, becoming aware of the heat again, the emotion quickly spent, he complained: 'But the new issue hasn't come yet.'

Then, 'Will you be here for much longer?' asked the doctor.

In English, 'You're not thinking of settling here *permanently?*'

'Oh no. Bonny's school begins next month, the university semester's also about to start again. Summer's ending over there.'

'Time flies,' said Dr Sen, again in English. 'We didn't really get a chance to talk this time—' Suddenly he smiled. 'All for the good though—I haven't had to make a visit! Admiral Chatterjee's and Mrs Chatterjee's health must be all right, touch wood, and you and your son seem to have got by somehow without falling ill.'

Dr Sen's visits were a form of socializing for Jayojit's parents. Last time, when the doctor had come to check Jayojit's father's blood pressure, they'd digressed into a conversation about mortality. It had begun with a discussion about the price of vegetables these days, and fish and prawns—the latter were almost prohibitive—and the price of meat. 'Tell me,' Dr Sen had asked, looking Jayojit up and down, 'do you eat a lot of meat?'

'I guess I grew up as more of a meat-eater than a fish-eater,' Jayojit had said. 'Though Bengalis claim that it's eating fish that makes them so brainy,' he laughed, 'it doesn't seem to have done any other part of their bodies much good. Anyway, why not say it?—I have to confess I've become quite dependent on junk food. Gone back to a second adolescence.'

'You know one thing,' the doctor had said, 'a lower middle-class Bengali's meal is one of the best a doctor can recommend. Low cholesterol, with harmless fish protein. It's cheap and it's good for you; you know certain kinds of fish fat are good for the heart. Anyway, I was reading somewhere,' he said (these doctors, even in semi-retirement, kept up with the latest medical journals), 'that Americans eat m-much less meat than they have ever before and have fewer heart attacks. On the other hand, heh,' he laughed, partly in embarrassment at his own amusement, 'Bengalis go there and find a plethora of meat, and eat much more of it than they ever have, and consequently die like flies.'

'I'm only an occasional steak-eater myself,' Jayojit said. 'I don't much go for huge chunks of red meat.'

The Admiral had interjected by grumbling: 'What's the point of living forever? Especially on a pension that can't keep up with inflation.'

This had met with great laughter, especially from the doctor, who'd responded to the Admiral's death-wish with, 'That's a good one, Admiral Chatterjee, but you mustn't deprive me of a job.'

That was then—an oasis of nervous banality in the midst of a time in which their lives took on another definition. Now Jayojit said:

'No, Bonny was all right. No sore throats or stomach infections. A slight allergy, but it was short-lived. I guess it was because we didn't move much out of the house. But,' he said in a fit of belated candour, 'I hope you'll find time to visit my parents soon. I worry a bit about my father's health—oh, I know,' he waved one arm and smiled without humour, agitated in his shorts and sandals, 'that it'll be all right as long as he takes care of himself—and God knows I have other things to worry about!' ('True,' murmured the doctor.) 'But I think they also need to *talk* to someone—don't we all! If you could just look after them while we're away—look after isn't the right word, of course, *look in* on them, rather, I'd be very grateful.' All this delivered in the serious public school accent in which he'd once addressed headmasters and countered competing debaters, and which he hadn't forsaken, or, rather, which hadn't forsaken him, and accompanied him through lecture rooms, domestic quarrels.

'Nischoi, nischoi!' said Dr Sen. 'I was anyway planning to visit them quite soon. And,' he lowered his voice to a confiding whisper, and looked around him once, 'the Admiral's health is all right, don't worry. He got a bit excited at the Building Society meeting—I can understand why. He should avoid excitement, *mental* excitement,' he widened his eyes, 'that's all. Let him,' he said casually, 'take an Alzolam to soothe him occasionally. No harm done.'

'He's always been rather excitable,' said Jayojit, looking back, for a moment, at his father's life. What he'd meant was that the Admiral had raw nerves; always in battle position.

'When will you come here again?' asked the doctor. 'How soon can you manage your next visit?'

'Around the same time I—we—came this year, I hope. Early April, in this awful heat.'

'Oh, very good!' said Dr Sen, and chuckled. 'Just in time for the mango season.'

'I hope things will have returned to normal by then,' said Jayojit in a public manner, not knowing exactly what he meant—eavesdropping, as it were, on his own words. He patted his stomach. 'Like my weight for instance.'

Jayojit's mother was in the kitchen. Tonight's leftovers would be eaten for lunch the next day; she would be too tired to cook again tomorrow. And once Jayojit and Bonny had gone in the evening, they—Jayojit's parents—would have a light meal of the daal and vegetables that Maya had cooked earlier. Time was being rearranged in their heads and their son's, connecting part of their life to another. Yesterday Jayojit had said, unusually for one who was quite formal about making requests of his parents, 'Oh for a fish that has no bones,' and so parshe had been brought; the fish lay on the pantry ledge, waiting to be fried.

'Better take this shirt down from here,' said Jayojit, getting up from the sofa; the shadow the electric light made of his body spread on the rug. A shirt was hanging from the clothesline. 'It seems to be dry now,' he said, touching it. He unclipped and took it down, giving it a look of protective recognition. 'Or else I'll forget it and leave it behind,' he said in explanation. He added: 'I'll iron it myself, later.' This little monologue, which he might have been directing to himself, was actually addressed to his father, sitting on a sofa before the television.

He folded the shirt, and, on the way to his room, picked up a worn book from one of the shelves; he weighed it as if it were an artefact. He laughed incredulously.

'What's this?' he said. '*Jackie*! Is this any good?' he asked, admiring Jacqueline Onassis's face a second time.

The Admiral looked up.

'Oh, your mother borrowed that,' he said, 'ages ago from the club.' There was a hint of accusation in his voice. 'Must return it. We'll have to pay the fine.' Just as the first touch of calm came to her from the early devotionals trickling in a small whine through the static on the transistor, these books on politicians' wives, some, like Margaret Trudeau, quite remote from her, once used to be part of the dream-life of her spare hours, while she'd be undaunted by four hundred pages of close English print.

Returning from the room, Jayojit said:

'Well, we didn't get to go to the club this time.'

'No,' said the Admiral. He seemed quieter than usual; he felt heavy and sluggish—as if in anticipation of the journey he would have to make in a couple of days, to the post office, to see why his pension cheque hadn't arrived at the beginning of the month.

'Maybe next time,' said Jayojit, flitting from shelf to shelf, checking for items he might have missed, picking up one of Bonny's prehistoric monsters: a pterodactyl.

He didn't like the club. He wasn't a member himself; and not being one, had to accompany his parents as a guest, a sort of overgrown child, allowed to sit with them but not to sign the bills or pay for the snacks and the drinks.

173

Reluctant waiters would come to take their orders, and, intermittently, people would drift through elegant arches towards their table to speak to his parents, spotting them under fans that hung from long rods, as they were passing. When they found out that he was a 'Non Resident Indian', some would squint with curiosity, as once people might have regarded holy men or charlatans. Two years ago, he'd been bent over a sweet lime soda next to his father when he'd been asked the tiresome question (he supposed it was unavoidable) by a man holding a glass of Club Cola in his hand: 'But, Mr Chatterjee, do you know Amartya Sen?' He'd stopped bothering telling people he was 'Dr Chatterjee'; Sen, supposedly introduced as a conversation-opener was, for him, a conversation-stopper. Really, he and Sen had nothing in common (given the fact that they were both Bengali, and economists), except that, now, they had had the experience of a failed marriage as well. Sen, with chastening resilience, had married again, while Jayojit was still trying to grope for a balance in the second phase of his life, and the idea of marriage seemed to him to involve too much spiritual effort. 'No,' he'd answered politely, perhaps a little abruptly, 'I met him at a conference twice—he may or may not remember me.'

Children were allowed to sit in the outer lobby of the club (they weren't allowed further inside) on a sofa, and here they played amongst themselves, not far away from portraits of the club's presidents, climbing on to the weighing scales. There was a children's room somewhere in the club, but Jayojit would never let Bonny sit there, while they ate and sipped fizzy drinks; this was another reason he hadn't been to the club this time.

Before Bonny was born, when he and Amala had gone there together with his parents, Amala would spend time observing the women; for the saris they wore were old-fashioned, the blouses clumsily made. 'Bengali women let go so easily,' she'd say. 'They become so otherworldly.' A woman would pass by, and Amala would glance at her hairstyle, and a smile would come to her eyes.

The club had recruited younger members since then. It had even opened a rather quaint barber-shop which no person in his right senses patronized. And, actually, Amala knew quite a few people amongst its members, certainly more than he did; 'Oh hi!' they'd say, 'How's mesho?' enquiring after her father.

The kitchen had been silent for the last five minutes; no more of the effervescence of the kodai; a smell of mustard-oil hung in the air.

'Bonny!' called Jayojit, craning his neck.

There was the customary silence before this cry registered itself.

'Yes, baba!'

'Come here!'

The boy ran out into the hall, still holding a pencil in one hand, suggesting he'd been interrupted in mid-performance.

'Want to go down and have a game of ping-pong?' Jayojit asked.

He'd bought a couple of racquets from a shop on Rash Behari Avenue.

'I don't know, baba.' He'd put one end of the pencil in his mouth.

Jayojit shrugged his large shoulders dramatically: 'Well, if you don't want to …'

The boy's face fell.

'Oh, go on,' said the Admiral.

But, downstairs, they found that one half of the table-tennis table had disappeared; the other half, with its pale green borders, remained, forlorn, truncated, a useless relic by itself.

'Oh no!' cried Bonny. 'Where's it *gone?*'

Jayojit looked around him, unable to conjure up the other half of the table. The table had been removed during the meeting, but he was pretty sure it had been returned to its place later. So absorbed had father and son been with their problem that they hadn't noticed the couple at the other end of the hall, who were walking a child. They had come closer now, an elderly couple in their sixties, led by a toddler of about two.

Following the child, the grandfather, a slight bespectacled clerical man wearing a brown shirt, his face averted but conscious of Jayojit's questioning gaze, walked leaning forward, but confident that his grandson could manage on his own, and that even if he fell, providence would keep him from serious hurt. Jayojit kept a half-smile of acknowledgement on his face, in case the man turned to look at him. 'Slowly, dadu,' said the man to the grandson. Jayojit didn't remember seeing them before.

Behind her husband, the grandmother walked more irregularly, a mass of confusions, now turning to look behind her, slipping her foot more firmly into her sandal, resuming her walk.

In the other room, his parents had gone to bed. He turned on the air-conditioner; it made a sound, like a throat-clearing, as machines sometimes do. Bonny was lying on his back, interlocking the fingers of both hands together, and, with a look of great concentration, prising them slowly apart.

'Better turn off the light,' said Jayojit, vacillating by the bedside. 'There's lots to do tomorrow.'

When he switched off the light, for a moment he could see nothing—the room disappeared. It never became so dark in the room in Claremont; some light, inquisitive and worldly, always entered through the curtains. The steady sound of the air-conditioner held him in his place; he began to make his way towards the bed, trying to imagine, from his memory, its location.

Jayojit overslept for some reason. Bonny strode into the room and admonished him in a dream: 'Oh, get up, baba, you're lazy.' He couldn't remember having had a dream—his sleep had been a blank; it had taken him to no other worlds. Rising swiftly, he turned off the airconditioner; it went off, with a sigh, like an afterthought. Inside the bathroom, he encountered a heat that had accumulated overnight and which the air-conditioning hadn't penetrated. Car horns could be heard until he turned on the tap; even then, over the water, a crow's cry reached his ears. Wiping his face with the towel, he raised his face and inhaled the dampness in the bathroom.

He emerged after brushing his teeth, and said to his mother in his lecturer's vernacular:

'And what's been happening in the interregnum?'

She didn't reply.

When Jayojit had just begun to read the headlines, Bonny said: 'Baba, tooth's shaking.'

It was the second time that this had occurred; as soon as he'd said the words, he opened his mouth, flashing his milk teeth, revealing the cavity that led to the source of his voice; with his eyebrows knitted, and a look slightly inebriated, he nudged the tooth with his tongue. It was a lower canine.

'I see it. Let it alone,' said Jayojit, seeing the sensation of the loose tooth could become a narcotic. 'You're becoming an old man,' he added, and sipped his coffee.

'Tamma, look,' Bonny said to his grandmother; she'd been hovering over a plant in the verandah, standing between it and the sunlight.

'O-o-oh,' she sighed dramatically, straightening and looking down at him. Yet her inside was pulled by a pain that was quite unlike that of the tooth, that had begun more than two years ago and would be with her now.

'You want to leave the tooth for thamma?' called Jayojit from behind the paper.

'Tamma,' asked Bonny, 'are all dadu's teeth *real?*'

'All are not real,' said his grandmother, watering the hushed flat-leafed plant, 'but some of them are real.'

'Like, he doesn't put them in a *glass?*'

'No, shona,' said his grandmother.

Maya came at about half-past ten and covered the bed in Jayojit's room with a Gujarati bedspread.

'Maya,' Jayojit said, turning to her, 'I'm leaving this evening. I've left your bakshish with ma.'

'When will you come back again?' she asked, with such innocence, as if he were going on a pleasure trip and she were as ignorant of this family's recent history as they were of hers.

'Ei—next year,' he said, looking back into the suitcase.

He didn't want a conversation now; he'd withdrawn into his private sphere where he meditated on a future that he didn't expect, or hadn't wanted, to confront. Turning his face toward her again, he instructed her, 'Work properly when we're away, and look after ma.'

His mother had complained to him again that every few days Maya pleaded absence from work, either because of some obscure excuse to do with the weather or the children's health, or because one of the innumerable local gods that presided over the poor—kitchen god, fertility god—had a Puja imminent and must be appeased. Given that his mother was exaggerating, he *had* noticed, in a dream-like way, Maya's impenetrable absences, and sensed that the laws governing her life were other than those that pertained to what he called 'ordinary' life.

Unmoved, Maya declared:

'Chhoto babu will be taller when he comes next time. He won't remember me.'

And I'll have a larger paunch, and you may not be in this job any more, thought Jayojit.

For lunch, they ate the parshe they'd had the previous night. Jayojit's mother had had Maya buy a packet of sandesh from a sweet shop. 'I know you like these,' she said. 'Take them with you. You or Bonny might want to eat one at the airport,' she added. 'For God's sake,' said the Admiral in English, 'don't bother him with trivial things at this moment!'

'No, ma's quite right,' said Jayojit. 'I do like sandesh. But there are customs officials at JFK who always keep an eye open for foreign-looking food, even fruit—you know, mangoes, custard-apples.'

'But these are harmless, Joy,' said his mother. 'They're unadulterated and good for you. Doctors prescribe them to their patients.'

'True,' said the Admiral, speaking from somewhere else.

'What will I do with these then?' she asked.

'Why—you and baba eat them! Have them with tea!' he said. 'I'll eat one now,' he said, and bit into a sandesh himself.

The Admiral abnegated the world and stole an hour-long nap, Jayojit's frequent conversations with his mother failing to wake him. By three o'clock, Bonny was dressed, and his pale feet, which had often padded about naked inside the flat, were hidden away inside socks and sneakers.

'I'm not gonna sleep tonight on the plane,' he warned his father. 'I'll watch the movie.'

'Of course you will,' said Jayojit; he was still in his shorts and sandals, as if he, at the last moment, had decided to stay back, or he were travelling to Barbados, and all he needed was a camera. 'Have you picked up your dinosaurs?'

'Uh-huh.'

'Your cars? What about your books?'

'I dumped them in the suitcase,' he said. 'But I want to take one with me, baba.'

'Okay. I'll put it in my bag,' said Jayojit. 'All right?'

There was a groan from the bedroom; the Admiral had got

up and realized what time it was. He slipped his large feet into his sandals and stumbled to the bathroom to wash his face. Meanwhile, Jayojit let the cover of the suitcase flop shut; and once more stood face to face with the tartan design against the blue background. He zipped it shut.

He whistled in the bath—he had obdurate dry hair, which didn't require frequent washing, hair peppered with a grey that seemed to be increasing almost daily. This metallic grey had come over him imperceptibly, and much fascinated his son, and pained his mother. Coming out of the bathroom, he said, buttoning his shirt, 'Fine: we're ready to leave. Where's Bonny?' Then, seeing the ragged heap of his old clothes—shirt, underwear, vest—he said 'Damn!' and had to bend down to open the suitcase again. Pressing them into a small bundle, he pushed them to one side, next to a much-perused copy of his book, *Ethical Parameters in Development*. The clothes passed like a cloud over the title. His laptop rested against his shoulder bag.

The Admiral had changed into another of his white shirts; hair carefully combed, he lumbered into the sitting room; he sat there as if he were a guest; coughed a couple of times, and glanced at his grandson in the verandah. Jayojit's mother had worn a starched tangail, and fastened her hair with a large clip. Jayojit dragged out the suitcase to the front door; it seemed to possess suddenly, after months of invisibility, a stubbornness and independence. 'Oof! It feels heavier than when we came here,' said Jayojit. To Bonny, he called, 'We're leaving!' Bonny took his eyes away from the bit of the lane he was watching and walked towards them.

Once they were downstairs, they were noted, without much interest, by a few schoolchildren returning home, in blue and white uniform, and probably commented upon.

'Right,' said Jayojit, 'I'm off to look for a taxi—only hope I can find one that isn't falling apart!' He strode towards the lane, followed purposefully by Bonny; his parents waited on the steps, the Admiral squinting through his bifocals.

They returned a few minutes later in a taxi; 'There's always one, thank God,' Jayojit said, getting out. A dog had begun to bark upstairs; not Mrs Gupta's pomeranian, but the Alsatian who lived on the first floor. The driver, a clean-shaven man in his early thirties, had looked after his vehicle well; the upholstery inside was clean, reflecting the sunlight, and the taxi's black and yellow shone brightly; he lifted the suitcase with a sullen respect. There was a companion sitting in the front—a boy in his teens, who watched with sleepy interest as the driver hauled the suitcase to the rear. The back of the Ambassador seemed to expand to accommodate the dour-looking grandfather, the grandmother, Jayojit, who, for some reason, was talking constantly, and Bonny, who stood between his father's legs, and when tired of doing so, sat down upon one of them.

As they turned into the main road and the building vanished from sight, the Admiral rolled down his window a little to allow a breeze that had reached the main road to run through his hair. He leaned back slightly.

'All right, baba?' asked Jayojit.

His father nodded. But they were caught in a traffic

jam in front of Modern High School, the massed cars still as a catacomb. Bonny turned to his father and whispered:

'Baba, who's that?'

A small cut-out of Hanuman, pasted to the bottom of the windshield, had caught his eye. Hanuman, above the two motionless wipers, was in mid-flight, holding a mountain above him: the Gandhamadan parbat.

'That's Hanuman, the monkey god,' said Jayojit, balancing the laptop on one knee.

'You mean, like, he's the god of the monkeys?'

'Well, yes, but let's say that he's a god who also happens to be a monkey,' said Jayojit.

'He must be *real* strong,' said Bonny, curling his lip and smiling knowingly.

A little later, as the traffic broke up and they turned into Park Circus, he asked his grandfather:

'Dadu, do you feel hot in that beard?'

The old man smiled and shook his head.

'I'm used to it,' he said. 'Like a dog is used to its coat.'

Then Bonny was largely silent, staring at the fleeting two-storeyed houses in by-lanes, the shops in Park Circus, the occasional outbreaks of shanty settlements, the thatched huts along the bypass; he was unmoved by the smell when they passed the rubbish dump, though his grandmother quickly pressed a handkerchief to her face.

By the time they reached the airport, the Admiral had been asleep for about twenty minutes; he woke up startled and bleary-eyed. Bonny was gone as soon as the taxi stopped, and returned brandishing a trolley, his chin above the handlebars.

'Okay, I'll take hold of the trolley, Bonny,' said Jayojit, after paying the driver. He checked to see if they'd left anything inside. 'No, that's fine,' he reassured no one in particular. Then, to Bonny, 'You can hold it at one end.' So, partitioning the responsibility of the trolley between themselves, they pushed their way inside.

Families were drifting around the hall, come to see off somebody. When the two, driving the wayward trolley, had finally reached the Bangladesh Biman counter at the extreme end of the check-in area, it was clear that there weren't many passengers, probably because of the time of the year. Jayojit joined a disjointed queue of three people; and there was another queue of the same number. Nothing else; all the other check-in desks unattended and closed. Visitors weren't allowed here; and, bereft of ordinary human society, the Biman passengers, who stood waiting with suitcases more imposing than themselves, had only their smiles and their passports (of two or three different colours, in their hands) to vouch for who they were. There was also something shabby about the walls and the small self-conscious trickle of international traffic, more like a leakage than a departure; yet almost each one of these people had lives they were going back to from the country they were visiting. The woman standing in front—an expatriate from the composition of her appearance; she was wearing blue jeans and vermilion in the parting of her hair, and a bindi on her forehead—turned her head and smiled at Jayojit. 'Going to Heathrow?' she asked, in a warm mixture of a Bengali and a London accent. 'No; New York,' he said. 'And you?' 'Oh I'm going to London,' she said, and laughed; she had slight buck teeth and striking long hair. The vermilion led Jayojit to briefly speculate about her husband, their children (if they had any), and their cold house and garden in the suburbs. 'A much shorter journey than mine, then,' he said. She shrugged politely, not knowing with what words to respond to his jovial but superior manner. After a while, he said 'Wait here' to Bonny, a picture of introspective ambivalence on the baggage trolley, and went off to pay the airport tax.

When he came back, he found Bonny still sitting on the trolley in a trance next to the suitcase. Jayojit looked around swiftly to see if there was anyone he recognized; there was always the risk, on Bangladesh Biman, of meeting someone you might have known casually in your past, of performing the usual surprised greetings, of slipping into small talk in a piecemeal hodge-podge of Bengali and English about some wedding you were to have attended or some ailment you'd recently had treated and explaining, in front of the checking in desk, your presence here at this moment. But he needn't worry, there was no one. He noticed a European woman, wearing a salwaar kameez, distinguishable from the others by her paleness, her brown hair, and her awkward, shy largeness.

Later, with only the laptop and shoulder bag on the trolley, Jayojit headed back with Bonny towards his parents; this time he let Bonny steer it. The hall looked large and outspread, as if it were being viewed through a lens; you couldn't see all of it at once. The airport itself, once both an international and domestic terminus, was undergoing some sort of subtle transformation since the new domestic airport had come into existence. The Admiral and his wife were sitting on the plastic chairs on the margins. They were eclipsed by a large family to their right—a widow wearing spectacles and a white sari, her middle-aged son and daughter-in-law, two young cousins, one of them holding a mineral water bottle, and a young couple and their child who, defined by some tension, some pull, that knit them more closely to each other than to the rest, were like an island gradually breaking away; it was clear that the rest had gathered to see them off. Between them they shared laughter and what seemed to the Admiral's ears like banal, nouveau-riche chatter; the kind of patois, increasingly heard, that combines the indecipherable new street-talk with the immemorial, histrionic platitudes of tradition.

'Well, that was much less difficult than I expected,' said Jayojit as he sat down next to his father.

'Everything done?' said the Admiral, shifting his focus.

'*I hope* so, sincerely,' laughed Jayojit, as he put the shoulder bag before him. 'The suitcase has gone—into the hands of God.' His father nodded, cross but almost sympathetic. 'There's news though—bad or good, I don't know—there's a half-an-hour delay. Apparently Biman has only one plane for its Dhaka-Calcutta flight, and that has a "technical fault" which can, however, be fixed.'

'"Technical fault!"' murmured the Admiral.

Bonny said: 'Baba, I'm going there'—he pointed to the centre of the hall. He ran towards the aquarium that had been kept there, pressed his nose against the glass while full-fed fish slid with oily stealth past his nose.

'Baba, ma, we can have a cup of coffee, you know,' said Jayojit; he'd noticed a boy in the distance, going around with a kettle in one hand.

'Coffee's too sweet here,' said his father, and shook his head.

But Jayojit's mother nodded: 'Coffee would be nice,' she said.

So Jayojit called the boy with the kettle, and he and his mother had coffee in plastic glasses, with a white froth swimming on the top, and it *was* much too sweet.

'I think I'll go and see if there's anything in the bookshop,' he said, getting up. 'Ma, see that he doesn't wander too far, will you?'

It was brutal, leaving them at this moment, but he felt he must do something, go somewhere; on his way to the bookshop, he became aware, for the first time, of the radiance of the electric lights above washing them all, and that it had become dark outside. What had been the domestic terminus lay partially deserted except for truant, bored children who'd trespassed there with nothing to do, and one or two bored adults as well; he passed an art gallery displaying a local artist's attempts at abstract expressionism, and a sort of crèche for mothers and children behind a ragged curtain. Entering the bookshop, he bent over the magazines, the faces of actresses, ministers, the dead who'd left the world surprised by an avalanche or stopped by a bullet, their faces printed with the last glow of life bright as the photographer's flash during the photo taken later at leisure. 'Tedious stuff,' he thought, picking one up dispassionately, 'all these indigenous *Newsweeks.*' A boy of about ten or eleven, his mouth open, was pushing a revolving bookrack in a leisurely way with his finger; Jayojit turned and stood next to him, attempting to read the titles of the turning books. 'Why do airports always have books by Raymond A. Moody Jr?'

At last, he decided to buy some chocolates, and a copy of the *Asian Age.* At the counter, he studied the objects under the glass and said:

'Two packets Nutties.'

Someone was watching him. It was a woman in a wheelchair, a widow in a white sari; someone had left her by the entrance to the bookshop. She too was going to make a journey; Jayojit's return of her gaze had no effect on her. She continued to stare at him, without hostility or friendliness.

'Twenty-four rupees.'

As Jayojit was paying for the Nutties, Bonny rushed into the shop:

'Baba,' he cried loudly. 'Dadu says do you want to get *left behind?*'

'Be with you in a second,' promised Jayojit.

The widow in the wheelchair smiled at Jayojit, in a way to suggest that they'd now been introduced.

The Admiral and Jayojit's mother had risen from their seats by the time Bonny and Jayojit had got back, and were looking blindly around them.

'Joy,' said his father, 'they've announced your flight twice already.'

189

'Let them,' said Jayojit, 'they won't leave without us.'

Through his bifocals, the Admiral was straining to make out the last bit of the departure area—which it wasn't possible to do. Piped music—a Tagore song on a Hawaiian guitar; he might know the words.

They came to the barrier where visitors must stop. Jayojit turned quickly and touched his parents' feet; then he rose and smoothed his shirt. A group of people at the barrier—two men, a woman in a cheap, shiny sari, the security man in khaki, holding a rifle—watched as he bent and rose again. 'Bloody idiots,' he thought. 'Nothing to do.' Another part of his mind was untouched by their presence. They watched as Jayojit's mother bent forward to hug Bonny, and eavesdropped on every word as she said to him:

'Bye bye, shona. Bhalo theko. You will write to thamma, no?'

'OK,' he said, nodding dolefully. He lifted his face to be kissed, reluctantly.

The bystanders smiled and watched as the grandfather now stooped to kiss the boy.

'Bye bye, dadu,' he said, and smiled a rare smile. 'Take care.'

Bonny forbore the invasion of the Admiral's warm beard into his face. Most of the onlookers had turned away; only one person continued to listen as Jayojit said:

'Baba, ma. I'll phone you once I'm there. Some time tomorrow.'

His father nodded.

In Dhaka, in the waiting lounge on the first floor, Jayojit dozed for half an hour; Bonny, meanwhile, watched MTV. Bonny and Jayojit occupied three seats; computer and shoulder bag, which Jayojit had laid on the seat in the middle, strategically separated father from son. This small separation was deliberate; it emphasized Jayojit's basic sense of security about his son, that he could afford to let Bonny and himself exist in partial independence from each other, that he could also fall asleep a foot and a half away from Bonny without worrying in his sleep. But Jayojit had also experienced a slight feeling of dislocation when he'd realized that, although they'd left Calcutta at half-past seven, it was still seven-thirty in Bangladesh. He'd put down laptop and bag with the knowledge that he'd been given this extra half hour which he must do something with. 'He moves, and he moves not,' he remembered moodily, reciting to himself, with grim satisfaction, the lines describing the Spirit in the Upanishads. 'He is near, and yet he is far.' He'd read the Upanishads in English when he was twenty-two, for, despite being a Brahmin, at least in name, he knew no Sanskrit.

Jayojit felt an unnatural hunger for the potato wafers they sold in the transit area. When he'd got up, he left Bonny in his seat and made a casual exploration of the lounge. Among the passengers was the Bengali lady he'd had a few words with, in a seat a couple of rows behind his. He sent her a smile of cordial, if non-committal, recognition, so important in these situations. A bespectacled couple were sitting in a corner, the man in a pin-striped shirt, silent. Further off, a long-haired woman wearing leggings was sitting by herself, her face inside a book. Walking to the glass windows on the left, he looked out, hoping to make out the colours of the landscape. But it was too dark. The glass was full of reflections—of seat covers, of women in shiny salwaar kameez outfits or in burkha, of children sitting on their mother's or father's laps.

Returning, he found that the European woman—the one in the salwaar kameez in Calcutta—was sitting opposite Bonny and talking to him.

'And you're going back to school?' she said. Looking up at Jayojit, she smiled and said:

'Hi! I'm having a chat with your son here. I remember you two from Calcutta!' The way 'Calcutta', on her lips, rhymed with 'rudder' revealed to Jayojit that she was American.

Sitting down, Jayojit said pointedly:

'Quite right; I remember you too. Actually, I couldn't help noticing you in your—ethnic garb.'

The woman laughed loudly and without reserve.

'They're very comfortable, aren't they? By the way,' she said, smiling at him and then at Bonny, 'I hope you don't mind me sitting here.'

'Not at all!' said Jayojit. He adjusted his glasses casually. 'Bonny and I were getting bored, weren't we? And old friends are welcome.'

'Oh, thank you!' she said. 'Where are you flying to, Mr—?'

'Chatterjee,' said Jayojit. 'Jayojit Chatterjee. We're going to New York, where we'll be forced to change planes.'

'Oh, I'm going to New York myself!' she said. Then she said mournfully to Bonny, tilting her head in mock apology: 'But I'm getting off there.' As if the next question led logically from this statement, she asked: 'I suppose you're Bengali, Mr Chatterjee?'

'Well—' said Jayojit, laughing, 'well, I guess you could say—well, yes—yes, I suppose I am!'

This confused answer seemed to have both puzzled and charmed Jayojit's companion; she laughed and said, after a moment:

'I'm North American, as you can probably tell. Boston born and raised. I was doing Salvation Army work in Calcutta ... for around three months. I loved it there. There's so much going for it, in spite of—you know'—she shrugged—'everything.'

People watched them as they walked past. Jayojit had never thought he'd like a Salvation Army worker if he ever met one; but now that he'd at last encountered one in the flesh, he found her neither pious nor complacent; and she was slightly plump, in innocent contrast to the poor she worked for.

'By the way, my name's Mary,' she said. 'I know,' she laughed, 'it's a really predictable name for someone who works in the Salvation Army, right?'

'Not at all ... I mean, I'm sure your parents didn't know you'd join the Salvation Army when they christened you.'

'That's true,' she said.

'What did you really think of Calcutta?' Jayojit asked. 'Was it too much for you?'

'I liked it!' she smiled, as if surprised herself. She had light brown eyes and the bridge of her nose had reddened with the sun. 'It's certainly like no other place I've been to! Next time I come I'm going to try and learn the language.'

Bonny was listening to this exchange with a half-smile.

'When's next time?' said Jayojit, as if there were a chance he might run into her in Calcutta—a slender hope, because he would not be ministering to the poor on his next visit. He felt not the slightest attraction towards her, and was reassured to sense that she probably felt none towards him.

'In a few months,' she said. 'Maybe in the summer.'

'Me too,' said Jayojit, surprised. He looked at Bonny. 'My son and I—Well, who knows?'

'Nothing wrong with these seats,' decided Jayojit, settling into his after pushing with brute force their hand-luggage and the laptop into the locker. Wearing his headphones, Bonny said: 'I'm a doctor!'

The ornate Bengali announcements startled Jayojit mildly; and Bonny remained tense and excited all through the take-off. Once they were in the air, he shouted to his father:

'Are we flying, baba?' He looked concerned.

'That's right.'

A woman came down the aisle with a tray in her hand; the aircraft was still tilted upward, and she made a cautious descent down the slope. Arms rose from the seats towards the glasses of orange juice. 'Thank you,' said Bonny to the smiling woman when he'd got his; they drank it eagerly—it was sour and bitter.

Getting up to go to the toilet, Jayojit looked round to see if there were any Indian Bengalis on the plane. There they were—

so easy to identify, myopic, the men slight and in nondescript Western clothes, the women betrayed by the telltale trace of vermilion in their hair. Surrounded by the Bangladeshis, with their large families talking loudly, many of the children already fast asleep, the women heavily bangled, trinkets shining on their ears and noses, young men in smartly tailored suits, old men with goatees.

When Jayojit had returned to his seat, Bonny said to him:

'Baba, this tooth's giving me *trouble!*'

'Is it?' he said. 'Don't prod it with your tongue, Bonny. You'll find, suddenly, that it's fallen off by itself.'

A man in a skull cap, with streaks of grey in his beard, rose unhurriedly from his seat.

A little later, Bonny took off his earphones and said: 'How long's it been, baba? An hour?'

Jayojit looked at his watch.

'Only twenty minutes, I'm afraid, partner,' he said.

'Only *twenty minutes?* You mean not even *thirty minutes?'*

'That's right.'

Later, Bonny asked:

'Is it an hour now?'

'Still twenty minutes to go.'

'Oh God!'

Jayojit unzipped his bag and took out the *Asian Age*. Beneath it, there was a lump of gur that his mother had kept aside in the fridge from March, wrapped in newspaper and stored in a polythene packet—she'd been firm in her belief that the American customs men would look upon it kindly and let it through. It was like a clod of earth—it would certainly confuse them. 'You mean you *eat* this?' they'd say. Far away at the back a boy was retching, and near Jayojit, in the same row, a woman in a sari was exhorting her child to sleep, while another, older child, looked on at her brother. He couldn't help listening to the woman. Although the paper lay open on his lap, he stared blindly at the cartoon of a rotund politician, and, turning a few pages, couldn't concentrate on what the editorial said about the decline of the Congress party. When the child became quiet after ten minutes, he looked at the cartoon with new eyes, made the sound of a laugh, and then decided to give the editorial a second chance.